'I'll make my fortune, no matter what I have to do . . .' Of all the desperate men who rush to dig for diamonds in the dust of Shelagh Maybury's South African farm, Luke Valentine, a handsome, disgraced Englishman, is the most ruthless. It's not long, though, before Shelagh comes to appreciate the advantages of having the biggest liar and cheat north of the Orange River on *her* land—for at least he protects her from lesser villains! Not that she can trust him an inch, even when she begins to fall in love with him. And surely his interest in her can only mean one thing? He must know something about her fortunes that she doesn't . . .

By the same author in Masquerade

COUNT ANTONOV'S HEIR
ZULU SUNSET

DIAMONDS IN THE DUST

CHRISTINA LAFFEATY

MILLS & BOON LIMITED
London · Sydney · Toronto

First published 1984

ISBN 0 263 10594 6

Set in 11 on 12 pt Linotron Times
08–0784–52,000

Photoset by Rowland Phototypesetting Ltd
Bury St Edmunds, Suffolk
Made and printed in Great Britain by
Richard Clay (The Chaucer Press) Ltd
Bungay, Suffolk

CHAPTER ONE

SHELAGH PLACED the carpet-bags on the ground for a moment, easing her aching muscles and rubbing her stinging eyes. Overhead the sun beat down mercilessly, and a vicious wind blew across the plains with their stunted scrub and spiny ridges.

Her heart contracted with terror and despair as she glanced about her. In all this alien space, this vast nothingness, there were only herself and her sick father and the surly Koranna driver of the four-ox wagon. No one to appeal to for help; no one to force the driver to stop until her father was better, or at least to allow Shelagh to ride on the wagon too, so that she could cushion him against the worst of the jolting.

The driver cared for nothing but his oxen. His conveyance had been the only one they could afford to hire at the railhead, and from the beginning he had made it clear that their combined weight and that of their luggage would be too much for the animals, except where the going was easy, so that Shelagh and her father would have to walk most of the way.

But two days ago, sudden savage rain had come down, drenching them to the skin within minutes.

Even though the rain had stopped as suddenly as it had started, Shelagh's father had caught a chill which had developed into a fever. While the Koranna had grudgingly allowed him to travel on the wagon, he had insisted that Shelagh should carry the heavy carpet-bags to compensate for the sick man's weight.

She picked up the bags once more and stumbled after the ox-wagon. There was still over a hundred miles to travel before they reached that far hinterland of the British Crown Colony of South Africa, that as yet unnamed spot at the confluence of the Vaal and Orange Rivers where a fabulous diamond had recently been discovered, luring fortune-seekers from all over the world ever since.

Their own humble wagon had long ago been overtaken by other, richer, conveyances which had been waiting at the railhead to charge inflated prices for bearing the hopeful and the greedy towards the diamonds. Shelagh had not the slightest expectation that they might catch up with someone else—someone who possessed medicines or knew how to treat a fever.

On and on the cattle-track stretched into the emptiness, marked out by the bleached bones of sheep and oxen which had perished on previous pilgrimages. In that dead, deserted landscape, Shelagh trudged wretchedly after the wagon, bowed down by the heavy bags, and fretted anxiously over her father. He was normally such a fit man, with such a zest for life. It was not like Jack Maybury to succumb to a chill . . .

At noon the driver shouted a command at the

oxen, and they came to a lumbering halt at a spot where the cattle-track adjoined a narrow stream. Before the rain, two days ago, the latter would have been nothing but a dusty gulley, but now red water foamed over stones, and the oxen bent their heads thirstily to drink. The Koranna began to build a fire to cook lunch, while Shelagh clambered up into the wagon to see her father.

She was shocked and terrified to find that he no longer recognised her. His fever-bright blue eyes focused on something beyond her as he muttered incoherently. His face was flushed and burning hot to the touch.

Shelagh jumped from the wagon to fetch a water-flask so that she could bathe his face, and then she stiffened in her tracks. At first she thought that her own despairing need had conjured up a mirage, so that the moving shapes on the horizon couldn't be real. But then she became aware that the ground beneath her feet was vibrating in a definite rhythm, and slowly she accepted that it truly *was* a wagon driven by a powerful team of mules which was approaching them, like an answer to a prayer.

It could only be another diamond-seeker, going their way. Hope and relief flared inside Shelagh as she waited. And then she realised that the driver had no intention of slowing down and stopping. After all, he had no way of knowing that they were in trouble, and already he had pulled out to overtake them in a wide arc.

His attention was wholly occupied in steering his team along a safe course between acacia scrub and stony outcrops, until he could rejoin the cattle track again ahead of the ox-wagon. And in that relentless wind it would be useless to shout to him for help.

Shelagh didn't hesitate. She gathered up her skirts and began to run as fast as she could along the cattle-track to cut him off.

He had rejoined the track now. She stood, gasping for breath and lashed by the wind, watching the mule-team thundering towards her.

If the wagon and mules had seemed like an apparition to Shelagh at first, she herself loomed up in front of its driver like some mystical being. He pulled hard at the reins, staring incredulously at her.

She stood head-on to the wind, so that her green cambric gown was moulded to her shape, uninhibitedly outlining rounded breasts, a tiny waist and long, slender thighs. Her hair had come down; dark red and heavy, it streamed out in the wind, framing a face with high, wide cheekbones, a small, straight nose and a determined chin. Violet-blue eyes between spiky dark lashes blinked up at him. She reminded him of a figurehead on the prow of a ship.

For a few seconds, as he brought the wagon to a halt, Shelagh had time to study its driver in turn. He had a strong face, with enigmatic brown eyes beneath heavy brows and slightly drooping lids. His mouth was wide and mobile, and curved slightly in a look which suggested that he was used to observing life with a certain cynicism. His hair was dark, and contrasted oddly with the maturity of his face, for it fell forward in an unruly quiff over his forehead, like that of a schoolboy. She judged him to be in his late twenties.

He jumped from the wagon, and simultaneously Shelagh moved towards him. 'Sir,' she said breathlessly, 'I am so very glad to have stopped you in time! My father is ill, and I have no medicine for him.'

'You could have been killed, appearing in front of the mules like that! Who are you?'

'My name is Maybury, sir. Shelagh Maybury.'

The unfathomable brown eyes studied her. 'What the devil was your father thinking of, bringing you along on such a god-forsaken journey?'

Shelagh stiffened. 'I go everywhere with my father. Besides, I couldn't have stayed behind alone in Sydney even if either of us had wanted it!'

'Australia . . .' the stranger mused. 'What did you say your name was? *Shelagh?*'

'I believe my father made it up,' she explained stiffly. 'He thought it sounded Irish, and as my mother was Irish, he felt she would have liked it . . .' She swallowed, and pocketed her pride. 'Please, could you help my father? He is delirious with fever, and I don't know what to do.'

He nodded. 'I'll turn round. Come, you'd better get up beside me, out of the way of the mules.'

He helped her into the seat beside him, and gathered the reins. She turned her head, and saw his slightly mocking gaze upon her.

'I take it,' he said, 'that you and your father are on the way to seek your fortune in diamonds.'

'Yes,' Shelagh returned defiantly, stung by the mockery. 'As, no doubt, you are too.'

He shrugged. 'I'm returning to the diamond-diggings, yes. By the by, my name is Luke Valentine.'

Within a short while the mules had halted beside the ox-wagon, and Luke Valentine was examining her father.

'We must get his temperature down,' he told Shelagh. 'Have some dry clothes ready for him. Your driver and I will carry him to the stream, and keep him in the water until we have reduced the fever.'

She stared at him. 'No! I won't allow such a thing! It would be fatal, coming after a chill—'

'You applied for my help,' Valentine said curtly, 'so unless you wish me to wash my hands of your affairs after all, kindly do as you're told!' His voice softened slightly. 'It really won't harm him, and hopefully it will do some good.'

There was nothing for it but to submit, however doubtfully, to the man's drastic treatment of her father. The alternative would be far worse, for there was something about Luke Valentine which warned her that he would be quite capable of driving away and leaving them there if she rejected his advice.

A while later, when he and the Koranna carried her father back from the stream, Shelagh was both surprised and greatly relieved to find that the ducking *had* benefited him, for he seemed more comfortable and not quite as delirious as before.

'I have some milk,' Luke Valentine said, 'which I bought yesterday from a passing goat-herd. That, mixed with brandy, would be the best possible medicine for your father at the moment. We'll put him in my wagon; the two of you can ride with me the rest of the way, while your driver follows on with your baggage.'

'I can't tell you how grateful I am—' Shelagh began.

Valentine dismissed her thanks with a gesture, and gave his attention to settling her father comfortably in the back of his own well-sprung wagon.

Shelagh unpacked a few essentials from their luggage, while Valentine spoke briefly to the Koranna, and took his place in the driver's seat, gathering the reins. Shelagh sat beside her half-conscious father, relief and anxiety warring in her mind. Of all the dubious adventures she had ever shared with Jack Maybury, none had been as fraught with possible pitfalls as this particular enterprise.

She thought of Sydney, on Australia's east coast, with its bays and promontories, its noble buildings and public gardens, and wondered if she would ever see any of them again. Not that life had always been easy or luxurious. Their fortunes had see-sawed perpetually; sometimes she and her father had stayed in the best hotels and dined on imported delicacies, and at others they had been plunged into the drabbest of lodgings where they were lucky to be fed watery soup.

Until she was about sixteen years old, Shelagh had accepted their shifting fortunes as normal, assuming it to be the pattern of everyone's life. She had never questioned the fact that they moved from place to place—sometimes in a great hurry, and with the utmost secrecy at dead of night. She hadn't given any thought to the fact that she was being brought up differently from most girls, or suspected that there was anything unconventional or dubious about their lives.

It was only during the past two years that she had realised the truth. Her father was an adventurer who had done something to cause his respectable family in England to cast him off. And because his tastes were too expensive for his income, he was perpetually seeking new ways in which to augment it. But this was his biggest gamble yet.

Shelagh glanced at her father, and smiled sadly. Ever since news had reached the world that an enormous diamond, weighing more than eighty-three carats, had been discovered in Southern Africa, Jack Maybury had been convinced that here at last lay the means of making his fortune. It didn't matter that he knew nothing of diamond-prospecting; fired with unquenchable optimism, he had begun to plan their departure for the Cape Colony.

'When I've found my own Star of South Africa,' he had told her, 'you shall have silk gowns and a carriage-and-pair, and we'll live together in a mansion which I'll have built for us!'

With a tender gesture, Shelagh leant forward to push the clammy hair away from her father's brow. In spite of their unorthodox existence, Jack Maybury had always done his best to shield her from the harsher realities of life, making some of their more desperate situations seem like a game to her. And no matter what their circumstances happened to be, he had never allowed any man to take the slightest liberty with her. To his family he might be a black sheep, but Shelagh knew that there was more to him than the faults and shortcomings for which the world judged him.

He had educated her himself to a standard far beyond that attained by better-bred young ladies, and had instilled his own particular set of principles in her.

'Never take advantage of anyone weaker than you, Shelagh,' he had told her. 'The strong are fair game. And talking of games, it's the winning that matters. Never let them tell you otherwise. And there are times when the only way to win is to fight dirty.'

She stretched herself out on the wagon beside her father. He might have fought dirty at times, she didn't know. But he didn't seem to her to have won at very much in life. And suddenly, as she stared at his unaware, feverish face, he seemed old to her for the first time, and she couldn't help wondering what would become of him when he grew too tired and spent for adventuring.

The thought was still hovering in her mind when sheer exhaustion overcame her and she gave herself up to the luxury of being driven in a well-sprung, comfortable wagon instead of having to walk, and she fell asleep.

She awoke to the realisation that they had halted. A rosy light streamed in under the wagon's canopy, showing her that her father now appeared to be sleeping normally. She moved to the flap of the canopy and looked outside.

The sun was setting, streaking the horizon with vivid shades of colour. A short distance away from the wagon, Luke Valentine had built a fire and was stirring something over it in a three-footed iron pot.

For some reason the almost domestic activity seemed to underline the intensely masculine quality of the man, and Shelagh was sharply conscious of him as she lowered herself from the wagon and moved forward to join him. She found herself wishing that she might have been able to do something about her hair, but she had forgotten to transfer the necessary ribbons and pins from the ox-wagon, and now she had no alternative but to allow it to fall unchecked to her shoulders. She must look like a hoydenish child, she reflected, instead of someone well past her eighteenth birthday.

Whatever Valentine might have thought about her appearance, he didn't show it. He glanced up at her, and said laconically, 'Supper.'

'Should we try and give some to Papa?'

He shook his head. 'The best thing we could do is to leave him to sleep undisturbed. If I gave you a blanket later on, do you think you could sleep on the ground beside the fire, so that your father may have the wagon to himself?'

'Mr Valentine,' Shelagh said drily, 'since we left Sydney I've been sleeping in the cramped steerage-quarters below decks of the ship; sitting bolt upright in the train bearing us from Cape Town to the railhead, and thereafter propped against the wheel of the ox-wagon. I assure you,

I could sleep *anywhere* after that!'

'Good. I think you'll find your father considerably better in the morning.'

Shelagh accepted a tin plate of stewed bacon and potatoes from him. Now that she was no longer consumed with anxiety over her father, the girl's appetite was healthy, and she ate with relish. After their meal Valentine made up the fire while she sat on the blanket, watching him.

A strange excitement was quickening in her veins, and it had something to do with the fact that she could not help learning something about this enigmatic stranger while sharing a whole evening alone with him.

But when he came to join her by the fire Shelagh herself was made to reveal all about herself, while his own secrets remained firmly locked behind those unfathomable brown eyes.

'I hope,' he began the conversation, 'that your father has independent means to support the two of you while he searches for that fortune in diamonds. Believe me, he'll need it.'

'He receives a regular income from England,' Shelagh began.

'He's a remittance-man, is he?' Luke Valentine hazarded with uncanny accuracy.

A deep flush stained Shelagh's cheeks. It had never mattered to her that her handsome, dashing, urbane father was a remittance-man whose wealthy relatives in England paid him to stay away. She neither knew nor cared what he had done to make his family banish him into exile and send him money regularly to keep him there. But that this stranger should have pigeon-holed him so accurately was humiliating.

'What—what makes you assume such a thing?' she demanded.

Valentine shrugged. 'Observation and instinct. The two of you are not of the usual flotsam and jetsam which has been streaming in after the diamonds. Your father was obviously a gentleman once, and he receives a regular income from England. But not a large enough income for his needs or tastes, or he wouldn't be here. He is clearly an adventurer, an irresponsible kind of man who thinks nothing of taking his young daughter with him on a dubious enterprise. And you were born in Sydney, of an Irish mother—'

Shelagh rounded on him furiously. 'Let me tell you something else, Mr Valentine, to add to your impression of my father! He and my mother were not married—'

'My dear child—' he began.

'I am not your dear child! My mother was a poor governess in Sydney when she met my father. She fell deeply in love with him. He didn't know that she was expecting his child. He returned to Sydney from one of his—his *adventures*, as you would no doubt term them, to find that she had died in childbirth, and that I had been placed in orphanage.'

Shelagh was forced to pause for breath. 'He had no need to do anything about the situation, Mr Valentine!' she went on fiercely. 'Scores of men, far more respectable than he, would have washed their hands of their illegitimate brat, but he lost no time in removing me from the orphanage! He took a house and hired a nurse for me, and he and I have been together ever since. And if you say one more snide thing about my father, Mr Valentine, I fear I shall forget that we are in your debt, and slap your face!'

In her anger Shelagh had jumped to her feet. Luke Valentine rose too, and grasped her by the shoulders, looking down at her. The firelight glinting on his face gave him a saturnine expression, quite at odds with his quiet voice, when he said, 'I do not judge your father, Shelagh.'

Something in his voice, together with his use of her name, produced a disquieting weakness inside her. But she forced herself to say fiercely, 'I did not give you permission to use my first name, Mr Valentine! I suppose you feel that the illegitimate daughter of a remittance-man has no—'

'Listen, you absurd child!' He lifted a hand to her chin, forcing her to meet his eyes. 'I make no judgment of your father. I, too, was cast off by my family. I, too, would have been a remittance-man if they had felt it necessary to pay me to keep my distance, and if I had needed to accept their money.'

Shelagh was about to ask what he had done to cause his family to disown him, even though something warned her that such a question would be unwise. But then, hesitantly and almost as if in spite of himself, his fingers began to move along the line of her cheek, exploring the silky texture of her skin.

She saw his eyes darken in what she recognised instinctively as desire. Her own heart had begun to beat tumultuously. She waited in breathless anticipation, her lips parted, and leant forward slightly until she could feel the hardness of his muscles against her own soft curves.

Suddenly and deliberately he moved away from her, and busied himself with the fire. He said curtly, 'I should get some sleep if I were you. We're making an early start in the morning.'

She lay, later, wrapped in her blanket, feeling bruised and humiliated and bewildered. She had wanted him to—*what?* Kiss her, she supposed. No one but her father had ever kissed her, and while she associated the caress with closeness and warmth, she had instinctively yearned for far more than that from Luke Valentine. And he had wanted whatever it was she yearned for, too, instinct told her. But he had rejected her. Why?

It must be, she decided at length, because he thought of her as a child. In her old washed-out cambric gown and with her hair falling to her shoulders, he could not have formed a true impression of her age. And short of abandoning all discretion and shame, and spelling out to him the fact that she was eighteen, there was nothing she could do to enlighten him. At least, not at present.

In the morning Jack Maybury was a great deal better. He was no longer delirious, and although still slightly feverish, was able to thank Luke Valentine for all he had done. When the mules were once more bearing them towards the diamond-diggings, Shelagh studied her father anxiously.

'You must not frighten me like that again, Papa.'

He smiled ruefully. 'I'm sorry, my angel.'

'Papa—' Shelagh hesitated. 'While you were so ill, I couldn't help wondering . . . If the need should ever arise, could your family in England be approached for assistance?'

He gave her a sad look. 'You'd better know the truth, my love. They want nothing to do with either of us, beyond sending my remittance.'

'*Either* of us? I thought they didn't know of my existence, Papa.'

It was a moment before he replied. Then he said quietly, 'I decided some months ago to write and tell them about you. They could have given you so much more than I could, Shelagh, if only they might have been persuaded to acknowledge you, and bring you out into London Society—'

'*Papa!*' Shelagh cried with horror. 'You contemplated sending me away, to them! How *could* you?'

He didn't look at her as he said, 'A girl needs more than just a father.' He broke off, and this time met her eyes, his own soft with tenderness and regret. 'But they don't want to know you, Shelagh.'

'Who cares about them?' she said defiantly. 'We're going to find a fortune in diamonds, and be rich, and we'll thumb our noses at them!'

He laid his hand on hers. 'That's right, my angel.'

Her father continued to make good progress, and apart from a troublesome cough became almost his old jaunty self. He and Luke Valentine struck up a male comradeship which excluded Shelagh. The two men rode up front together, and even when they stopped to make camp the conversation was almost exclusively about diamond-mining.

Shelagh tried, subtly, to extend the scope of the conversation, and somehow convey her true age to Valentine. But he appeared to have lost interest in her completely, which only sharpened her own interest in him. She listened to the two men in piqued silence.

Valentine, she learnt, had experience of diamond-mining in India, and he had sunk a lot of capital into buying equipment to test a theory of his own.

'Diamonds are formed inside volcanic pipes,' he explained, 'usually found in river-beds. But it stands to reason that some of those pipes must still exist in watercourses which became silted up through the ages, and dried out centuries ago. In other words, diamonds could be found anywhere other than in flowing rivers, if only one knew where to dig for them.'

As the mule-wagon drew nearer to the diamond-diggings, traffic was joining them from all directions, bringing all kinds of conveyances, all kinds of people on a mass migration in search of a dream.

The diggings themselves came as a rude shock to Shelagh. She had expected a colourful place filled with drama and excitement. Instead, the squalid encampment of haphazard tents and mud and corrugated-iron shacks stretching away from the banks of the Orange River seemed merely ugly, overlain with an atmosphere of unfulfilled hopes and dreams turned sour.

A few small diamonds had been found, but nothing so far to justify the greed and the optimism which had brought all these people to the diggings.

Jack Maybury refused to be depressed, and as soon as he had set up the tent which Luke Valentine negotiated for him to buy from one of the traders, he went off to join the diamond-seekers along the river bank.

Shelagh stayed behind in their tent, and kept house as best she could. But everything, even the most basic commodity, was at a premium at the diggings. A humble cabbage cost a half-sovereign, and provisions like sugar and tea were impossible luxuries. But even apart from her domestic difficulties, she found life flat and unsatisfactory.

This feeling had more to do with Luke Valentine than with anything else. She knew that her father saw him almost daily at the river, but he never came to their tent. Sometimes she caught sight of him in the camp; tantalising glimpses which fed her interest and her frustration.

She began to weave fantasies about him. The ox-wagon had arrived with their luggage, and each day Shelagh chose her gown with care, and dressed her hair in a sophisticated style, and prayed that today would be the day he chanced to call at their tent and see her with new eyes. But he never came, and unfamiliar emotions and strange longings brooded inside her as she strove to create a semblance of normality in that alien, coarse settlement.

She tried hard to ignore the roughness of the life at the diggings, the fights which broke out nightly, the shrewish, disillusioned women who struggled to make a home for their families in that shanty-town. She tried to take comfort from the fact that her father had found a physician in the camp, a Dr

Paul, who was treating his stubborn cough.

One late afternoon Shelagh could no longer contain her strange obsession to see Luke Valentine. Her father would not be coming home until after sunset, when it grew too dark for him to examine the concentrate washed from the river for signs of diamonds. She would walk out to meet him, and contrive to take a path which led past Luke's tent. It would be the greatest ill-luck if she did not run into him.

But first she made careful preparations, choosing her dark-rose foulard gown with its white muslin *fichu* trimmed with Breton lace which set off her shoulders so well. Then she arranged her hair in a cascade of curls tumbling from the top of her head, held in place with a ribbon.

The sun was setting, lending the settlement a rare illusion of beauty as its rays turned the dust in the air to shades of brilliant colour. Shelagh was picking her way between the tents and shacks when she realised that a great deal of noise was coming from one of the shacks in her path. As she drew level with it, a man emerged from inside, weaving as he walked. Now she remembered that her father had said some of the more desperate women distilled rough alcohol from maize and sold it to the diggers to make ends meet.

The next moment the man had lurched forward and was grinning drunkenly at her. Before she could evade him he had grabbed hold of her shoulders, pulling her towards him.

She fought furiously, kicking at his shins, clawing at his face before her hands were imprisoned behind her back. A crowd of other men had appeared from the shack, attracted by the noise, and were egging on her attacker. She could smell the man's sour breath as he sought her mouth, and a wave of revulsion seized her. She closed her eyes.

Suddenly she was free, staggering slightly, and her tormentor lay on his back. Luke Valentine loomed menacingly over him.

Shelagh was shivering with reaction. Luke uttered a last threatening growl at the crowd before he took her arm in a firm, ungentle hold and marched her away to his own tent.

As the flap fell into place behind them, everything but his nearness was blotted from Shelagh's mind. She moved towards him, her heart thudding tumultuously, her lips slightly parted in unconscious invitation.

She had no artifice, no coquettish tricks. She recognised now what had been happening to her, and it did not even occur to her to try and hide the fact that she had fallen violently in love for the first time in her life.

She saw his eyes darken in response. He made a movement towards her, and checked it, biting off an oath. 'What the devil do you think you're playing at?' he demanded roughly. His arms were rigidly by his sides, his hands balled into fists.

'I—beg your pardon?' She blinked at the ferocity and unexpectedness of the attack.

'Look at you! You deserved everything you got! What did you imagine would happen when you set out deliberately to flaunt yourself in a place like this?'

'I—I wasn't flaunting—'

'No? Then what was the reason for parading round a rough mining-camp in such a provocative gown? You're not so innocent that you couldn't have foreseen what effect you would have on the diggers!'

Her lips trembled. 'I—I didn't think of them. I just wanted you to see me in my best gown—'

She heard him make a raw sound. 'You thought I was a child,' Shelagh went on painfully, 'and I wanted to show you—'

'I have never needed any physical evidence,' he said with a certain grim emphasis. 'Not since the first moment I clapped eyes on you.'

'Oh . . .' She looked at him uncertainly. 'If you don't think of me as a child, then—then don't you want to—to kiss me?'

'No!' His voice held a curious, rasping sound.

She tried hard to control the trembling of her lips. 'I see . . .'

For a moment he met her eyes, a blank and unreadable expression in his own. Then he took off his coat, and said flatly, 'You'd better wear this over that eye-catching gown. Go straight home, Shelagh, and keep out of trouble.'

As he laid the coat over her shoulders her hands came up, almost as if she had no control over them, imprisoning his and sliding them down her bare throat to the curve of her breasts.

He made a tormented sound. *'Damn you—'*

'I don't understand,' she whispered, very close to tears. 'I don't know—what to do to make you like me. Is it—is it that I'm not pretty enough?'

He jerked her against him then, so that the coat slipped from her shoulders to fall on the floor. His mouth covered hers, possessing her senses, setting the blood leaping in her veins. It was her first experience of physical passion and yet it was somehow totally familiar, and she moved against him, intuitively employing little female tricks which she had never suspected she possessed.

'I love you,' she murmured, when he lifted his mouth from hers.

He was utterly still for a moment. Then, with a rough movement, he picked her up in his arms and threw her down on the truckle-bed, pinning her body down with his own. There was no hint of tenderness in him as before. His mouth came down upon hers in a kiss which was brutal and deliberately savage. When she began to struggle his hands ripped at the bodice of her gown and she felt his hands upon her breasts, bruising her flesh in what had become something which couldn't be described as anything but an assault.

She succeeded in freeing her hands and she beat at his chest. He let her go, heaving himself from the truckle-bed and pulling her to her feet as well without gentleness.

Tears were coursing down her cheeks. She could taste the blood seeping from a cut in her lip where it had been forced against her teeth by his punishing kisses.

'Why are you crying?' he asked coldly. 'What did you expect to happen when you threw yourself at me? This is real life, and not some romantic fantasy. Grow up, Shelagh. If you want to prove that you're not a child, stop inflaming men's passions and playing silly games of love.'

She turned blindly away, her only thought to escape. But as she left the tent and the cool evening air struck her bare shoulders she was reminded of the state of her gown. Even in the depths of her humiliation and pain she knew that she could not risk passing through the camp in a condition of undress, and she was forced to return for Luke's coat.

He was seated on the truckle-bed, his elbows resting on his knees, his head sunk in his hands. As Shelagh grabbed the coat from the floor, where it had fallen, a part of her mind registered gratitude that he appeared to be unaware of her return. Then, wanting only to remove herself from the scene of her degradation, she dismissed the thought and fled from the tent.

She said nothing to her father of the incident, but allowed him to assume that her gown had been ripped during her encounter with the drunken digger. She was almost grateful now for the drunk, for she had no further need to explain her bitter tears or her state of complete emotional shock. Jack Maybury asked no awkward questions, but comforted her and petted her and kept his arm about her heaving shoulders until she had cried herself to sleep.

In the morning when he set out for his claim at the river she felt drained of all emotion. Even when he returned unexpectedly, only an hour or so later, she experienced no curiosity or alarm, but simply looked at her father with dull eyes.

'We're leaving the diggings for a while, Shelagh,' he said quietly.

'Oh. Where are we going, Papa?' she asked without much interest. Nothing seemed to matter any longer.

'We're going to become paying guests of the Widow Steenkamp, who owns a farm just beyond the Griqualand border.' He came to sit beside her. 'I've been thinking of it for some time, my angel. It was Dr Paul who first suggested it, because of this wretched, persistent cough of mine. He believes that farm air will have a beneficial effect, not to speak of a diet of fresh butter and eggs and the like. And I also feel that you should have a chance to recover from your ordeal of last night. I have therefore been making the necessary arrangements.'

'When do we leave, Papa?' Shelagh asked listlessly.

'There's no time like the present. I have hired a wagon and driver, so we must pack quickly. The journey to Mooifontein, the widow's farm, will take us all of four days.'

Submissively Shelagh began to pack their possessions on the wagon. Their departure from the camp created no interest; everyone was too intent on chasing his own dreams of a fortune to care about the comings and goings of others. Shelagh did not see Luke again.

They reached Mooifontein towards the end of the fourth day. The sun was just setting, touching the bleak countryside with its endless, rolling veld with rose and gold. The farmhouse nestling in a slight dip seemed scarcely better than one of the shacks they had left behind them. Flat-roofed, built of red mud, with small, mean windows glinting like malevolent eyes in the dying rays of the sun, it appeared singularly uninviting to Shelagh as they approached.

She could not, however, fault the welcome which Maria Steenkamp gave them. Their hostess was a plump, youngish woman with a shy smile and gleaming black hair which she wore in a coil in her neck. She spoke English quite well, and assured them that they could stay at the farmhouse for as long as they wished.

'It must be a relief to you to get away from those terrible diggings!' she said, calling her three children to be introduced to the guests. The two boys were twelve and thirteen respectively, and their sister ten. None of them could speak more than a few words of English; they all seemed sullen to Shelagh, and she thought they resented the interlopers.

But there was no doubt that life on Mooifontein seemed to suit her father. He appeared not to mind the bleakness of the setting, and he threw himself with apparent enthusiasm into the daily chores of the farm. He chopped wood for the widow, and allowed her to teach him how to milk the scrawny cows. He had slipped quite quickly into an easy relationship with Maria Steenkamp, and Shelagh could often hear the widow laughing helplessly at some joke of her father's.

She wished that she could have been equally contented. But kind though the widow was,

Shelagh had nothing in common with her or her children. And the monotonous tenor of life on the farm stifled her. She could not escape the feeling that too many days of her life were wasting away uselessly.

In spite of everything, her treacherous heart longed for Luke. The numb shell about her feelings had long since cracked, and the instinct to go to earth like a wounded animal had left her. She wanted the chance to live again, to fight again, even to lose again if she had to.

More than anything, she wanted to see Luke again. And even if he continued to repulse her, even if she had to endure humiliation and pain from his nearness, it would be preferable to being buried alive on Mooifontein, merely existing, marking time.

One evening when she was helping her father to drive the cows home for the milking, Shelagh appealed to him. 'Papa, surely it is time that we should think of leaving Mooifontein and returning to the diggings?'

He did not answer immediately. When he spoke his voice was drained of all emotion. 'We're not leaving, Shelagh. Not ever.'

'Papa!' She stared at him, appalled at the unthinkable notion of being trapped, a paying guest for ever, on Mooifontein. 'Whatever can you mean?'

He took her hand in his, and looked down at it for a moment. Then he met her eyes. 'There is something you must know, my dearest. There is far more wrong with me than just a persistent cough.

In fact, not to mince matters, I am dying.'

His words echoed in her ears, making little sense. 'No,' she whispered. *'No!'*

His fingers tightened about hers. 'That is why I took you away from the diggings, Shelagh. I could not risk dying in that terrible place, and leaving your fate in the hands of Luke Valentine.'

Shelagh gave him an agonised look. Since he was wrong about Luke having any interest in her fate, he must also be wrong about his own condition. She clung to the thought, and shook her head. 'I am nothing to Luke, Papa—'

'No, and that is how I wish matters to remain.' Jack Maybury's voice was grim. 'I saw Luke the morning before we left the diggings. I returned his coat, and thanked him for rescuing you from the drunk, and then he told me what had occurred between you. To his credit, he tried to protect you from yourself. He used you brutally, hoping to kill the feelings you have for him.'

Through the awful chaos in her mind, one previously suppressed memory began to surface. That of Luke, sitting on the camp-bed with his head in his hands, as if he were in despair. And he had misused her for her own sake. His reasons were obscure, but surely it meant that he cared a little for her?

'But he is only a man, after all, and not a saint,' she heard her father go on, 'and by the morning he'd had second thoughts. He put before me a proposition—Well, you are too young and innocent to understand—'

'Are you hinting that he wanted to make me his

mistress, Papa?' Shelagh asked slowly. 'You must have misunderstood! He must have been talking of marriage—'

'No, Shelagh,' her father said, looking at her with sorrow and tenderness in his eyes. 'He was not talking of marriage. He could never do that. He already has a wife.'

CHAPTER TWO

IT WAS as if one blow after another had rained down upon her head, each devastating in itself but having the accumulative effect of finally knocking her senseless. Shelagh felt her legs buckling beneath her, and dimly heard her father cry out.

When she regained consciousness it was to find that he had carried her to the meagre shade cast by a giant antheap. *He couldn't have done that*, was her first coherent thought, *if he really were dying . . .*

His face swam before her gaze. He looked as dapper and dashing as always with his waxed moustaches, his flowing cravat and his thick dark hair parted in the middle. His complexion had a healthy, open-air ruddiness. How ridiculous to believe for one moment that there was more the matter with him than just a troublesome cough!

He had allowed himself to be frightened by Dr Paul—that's what it was. Dr Paul—scarcely a shining example of the medical profession! How could one place any value on the opinion of a doctor who would give up his vocation for the lure of diamonds?

Shelagh had always thought him a disreputable-looking little man, his waistcoat invariably stained, his fingernails none too clean. He probably drank too, judging by his high colour. He could never have been a very good doctor in the first place, or he would not have been persuaded to try and make his fortune in the squalor of the diggings. His opinion was worth precisely nothing! It had all been a panic-stricken nightmare . . .

Shelagh sat up from her slumped position in the lee of the antheap. Her father loomed over her, regarding her with contrition.

'I should not have blurted out one shock after another in that way, my love. Indeed, I had fully intended to keep from you altogether the fact that I am dying—'

'Papa—' She caught his hand in hers. 'I am sure that you are nothing of the kind! Why, you have only the word of that dreadful little Dr Paul! How could you have listened to him? In all probability he coveted your claim at the river, and sought to be rid of you!'

'Shelagh, my dearest, listen to me—'

'No, Papa, it is *you* who must listen! You were ever used to exaggerate in your mind any little ailments which befell you. You know you were! So when Dr Paul told you what he did, whether out of malice or incompetence, you foolishly believed him! But anyone with the least bit of sense could see that you are in positively radiant health! Why, you don't even cough as much as you used to! Confess that you don't!'

Jack Maybury hesitated, and then shrugged. 'Yes, it is true that I cough less often.'

'And your appetite has improved—'

'Yes.'

'You see? You must put these morbid thoughts from your mind, Papa, and let us return to the diggings.'

'Shelagh.' Her father's voice was quiet. 'You wish to return to the diggings because of Luke. You must accept that he is married.'

Thoughts which she had been keeping at bay crowded in upon her, robbing her of comfort, laying her waste to dull misery. *Luke had a wife.*

'I—do accept it, Papa. But—we made too many sacrifices to reach the diggings, you and I. We cannot allow anyone or anything to keep us from searching for those diamonds which are to make our fortune. I shall—put Luke out of my mind . . .'

Her father squeezed her hand in silent compassion. She looked up at him, and whispered painfully, 'If Luke is married, Papa, then why is his wife not with him? Where is she?'

'In England, Shelagh.' Jack Maybury was silent for a moment, and then said abruptly, 'I think I had better tell you the story as Luke told it to me, and then you must forget him. I believe you know that his family have disowned him?'

'Yes—'

Her father came to sit beside her, and placed an arm about her shoulder. 'Luke comes from a prominent, well-connected family, one which moves in the best London circles. When he was only twenty-one, he fell in love with a Society beauty. He thought his case was hopeless, for every other young man of standing was in love with her too.

And then, to his unbelieving joy, she began to encourage his advances, and when he proposed marriage, she accepted.'

Shelagh sat motionless, allowing raw pain to wash over her, mixed with such savagely bitter jealousy as she had never before experienced.

'Theirs was acclaimed the wedding of the year,' Jack Maybury went on, 'It was not until after the ceremony that Luke discovered the truth. He had been duped into marrying her by a conspiracy between his bride and advisers to someone close to the throne.'

'I don't understand,' Shelagh protested, frowning.

Her father sighed. 'No, I'm sure that you don't. You have led a life completely sheltered from that kind of sophisticated cynicism. You see, my dearest child, if a prince of the royal blood wishes to conduct an affair with a Society lady, then an elaborate smokescreen of respectability has to be created behind which to shelter. It is necessary for the lady to be married, so that the prince can claim friendship with both her and her husband.'

Shelagh made an involuntary sound of shock, and her father continued, 'The husband is required to turn a blind eye to what is going on between his wife and the prince, and in return many favours are granted to him and his family. Indeed, most husbands deem it an honour to be of such service to royalty, and many a knighthood has been conferred in the past for that kind of complaisance. That has been the accepted order for centuries. But Luke would not accept it.'

'No,' Shelagh agreed slowly. 'No, he *wouldn't.*'

'He caused a tremendous scandal within high Society circles by abandoning his bride as soon as he discovered the truth. His family dissociated themselves from his behaviour by disowning him. He was forced to leave England and find his living as he might.'

'Papa—' Shelagh looked at Jack Maybury with dawning hope. 'This marriage of Luke's, then, is no marriage at all. I remember reading in the English newspapers which reached Sydney that more and more Society couples are obtaining annulments or divorce—'

Her father shook his head. 'That is out of the question in this case. If Luke were to attempt such a thing, he would have to name the royal prince in his petition. The establishment would immediately close ranks to protect the prince, and give the lie to Luke's allegation. All that would be accomplished would be his family's utter social ruin as a result of the further scandal.'

'But she—the wife,' Shelagh said desperately. 'Surely she cannot wish to cling to what is not truly a marriage, and which does not even provide her with the respectable façade she sought in the first place? Could she not be persuaded to seek an annulment on the grounds that Luke deserted her?'

'When all of London Society knows *why* he deserted her?' Jack Maybury returned drily. 'She and the prince would be lampooned, made a public laughing-stock. No, my dear. She would do nothing to draw further attention to the situation.'

'Then he is well and truly trapped for life,'

Shelagh whispered with bleak despair.

'Yes, my poor child. And you must put him out of your thoughts.'

Shelagh glanced about her, at the endless lonely expanse of the veld. 'If I promise to do so, will you promise to return to the diggings, Papa? I am convinced that there is nothing seriously amiss with your health.'

Jack Maybury did not answer at once. His gaze appeared to be fixed on some distant horizon. 'Very well,' he said at last. 'When I have not coughed at all for three consecutive days and nights, we shall return to the diggings.' He stood up. 'Come, now, let us drive the cows home. Maria will be wondering what has become of them and of us.'

Shelagh tried after that to live through each day at a time, and marvelled at the fact that her father could ever have believed he was dying. His zest was such that he had even begun to forge a relationship with the widow's three children, teaching them English, playing games with them when he was not joking with their mother or helping her with the farm chores.

For her own part, Shelagh found the children stolid and dull. Hannes and Dirkie, the two boys, seldom had a word to say for themselves. Their sister Rina was a pretty enough little thing with a disconcerting habit of following Shelagh at a distance and then taking flight when she was spotted. And with their mother Shelagh had no affinity at all. She waited with growing restlessness to leave the farm.

On Mooifontein, where she had more than enough time to think, it was beginning to dawn on Shelagh just how much her father had always sheltered her from the realities of life. Perhaps *because* she was the illegitimate daughter of a remittance-man and his mistress, he had fought fiercely to guard her against any potential moral hazards. Unorthodox as their life together had always been, he had never allowed her to be placed in a situation where she might have had even a light flirtation with a young man. Perhaps if he had, she would not have fallen so completely and agonisingly in love with Luke.

Luke. It was impossible, of course, to keep her promise to her father and put him from her mind. Indeed, she took what comfort she could from the knowledge that he had wanted her enough to propose making her his mistress. And daily she began to suspect more and more that the real reason why they were continuing at Mooifontein was because her father wanted to keep her away from Luke.

Life was insupportably dreary on the farm. The only event of the slightest interest was the visit of an itinerant trader on his way to the diggings with a wagon-load of supplies. The trader stayed overnight on Mooifontein, and Shelagh felt bereft as she watched him depart once more. In four more days he would be where Luke was . . .

She was beginning to listen obsessively for her father's cough, keeping an account of each paroxysm. He continued to look so well otherwise, with such a good colour, that she could not help suspecting that he induced the coughing attacks deliberately, as a means of keeping her on Mooifontein. It did strike her that he had lost weight, but since he was throwing himself so wholeheartedly into the farm work that was not surprising.

One afternoon, as Shelagh sat on the *stoep* of the farmhouse, watching the tumbleweed blowing across the bleak veld on an aimless journey to nowhere, her father came strolling towards the house from the barn, his arm affectionately about Maria Steenkamp's shoulders.

'Dearest,' he addressed Shelagh, 'Maria and I have happy news to impart.'

'Yes, Papa?' she replied politely. One of the cows had been ailing; her father was becoming so immersed in the details of the farm that she had no doubt he was about to report its recovery.

Then she noticed that his eyes were not in the least happy as they rested upon her; rather they were shadowed and uneasy. But he spoke with forced cheerfulness. 'I have asked Maria to be my wife, and she has done me the honour of accepting. The Boer ceremony of *Nagmaal* is about to take place on the de Beers' farm, and we will ask the minister to perform—'

'No . . .' Shelagh cried, coming out of her trance of horror and disbelief. *'No!'* Her voice rose to a shout.

'Shelagh!'

She gathered her skirts and fled, running across the veld in a mindless rejection of everything her father's news had meant. He caught up with her and forced her to a standstill. Two spots of bright colour glowed on his cheekbones and his breathing was laboured.

'Shelagh, listen to me—'

She began to beat impotently at his chest with her fists, tears of utter hopelessness rolling down her cheeks. He caught her hands in his.

'Your behaviour was very hurtful to Maria, my love,' he began.

'I don't—care! How *could* you, Papa?'

She heard him sigh. 'I am marrying Maria for many different reasons, Shelagh. But the most important reason is that, by doing so, I shall be providing you with a mother.'

'I don't want a mother! I have never—felt the lack of one! You promised we would go back to the diggings! *You promised*, Papa!'

'I qualified that promise, remember?' His voice was quiet. 'I said we would go back if I had not coughed for three consecutive days and nights. I knew it was a promise I would be unable to keep. You would not allow yourself to believe it, Shelagh, and I allowed you to cling to your illusions for as long as I could. The truth is that I really am dying.'

She grew still, and stared at him. 'Dr Paul—'

'Dr Paul only confirmed what I began to suspect even when we were still in Sydney, my love. It was because of my suspicions that I wrote to my family in England and asked if they would take you in. They not only refused but also made it clear that my remittance would end when I died. They did not recognise any responsibility towards you.'

Shelagh tried to speak, but her lips had grown numb. Her father touched her hair with a gesture of sadness.

'At the beginning I didn't want to believe what was staring me in the face, Shelagh. And yet I knew that I had to make provision for you. I clutched at the idea of finding a fortune in diamonds. So I brought you to Africa, ignoring the possibility that I might die without finding that fortune and leaving you in even more dire straits.'

Jack Maybury sighed deeply. 'When I fell ill on the journey to the diggings, I was forced to realise what a fool I had been. I tried to hide my symptoms from you for as long as I could, but the fever I could not hide. When I recovered from that, I knew that time was slipping away from me. And at the diggings I saw how appalling the results would be for you if I died there.'

Shelagh brought his hand to her mouth, and tasted her own salt tears as they dripped on it. She was still unable to say anything.

'I could not risk dying at the diggings, my angel,' her father continued. 'It was Dr Paul who told me about Maria Steenkamp. He said she was a motherly, warm-hearted woman who was desperately lonely, and who would almost certainly marry the first personable man who offered for her. So, after I spoke to Luke Valentine that morning, I decided to bring you to Mooifontein without further delay, and ingratiate myself with Maria so that she would consent to marry me.'

'Does—does she know?' Shelagh managed.

'She knows that we will not be together for long.

I could not have hidden my illness from you so effectively if I had not had her help. But she does not know that I set out deliberately to marry her, and it would be kinder not to let her find out, for she loves me. She has promised to be a mother to you, my dear, and to look after you when I am no longer here.'

He broke off as a fit of coughing seized him. When he was able to, he went on, 'You will be safe here, my child. This will be your home from now on, Maria and the children your family. Here on Mooifontein you will never be exposed to the pitfalls and the dangers life can hold for a young girl in your situation.'

He could not possibly know that his words, intended to comfort and reassure her, only compounded her terrible grief and showed her a future as deadly to the spirit, and as bereft of all hope, as an indefinite prison sentence.

The next day everyone from Mooifontein began to journey by ox-wagon to the neighbouring farm, Vooruitzicht, which was owned by the two de Beer brothers, so that Jack Maybury and Maria Steenkamp could avail themselves of a minister's services and be married.

Nagmaal, Maria explained gently to a silent and withdrawn Shelagh, was a religious meeting of the Boers dedicated to the Last Supper. Because of the scattered isolation of the farms it was not practicable to have a church built for communal worship, so minister and congregation gathered instead on one of the farms for a week of services. It was also a social occasion, one of the rare times when far-flung neighbours were able to meet. And, Maria confided blushingly, there were usually two or three couples who took the opportunity to be married after *Nagmaal*.

For the first time, Shelagh really troubled to study this woman who was soon to be her mother. Maria had put on weight during the past months, perhaps because she now had a man to love and to help her with the heavier chores on the farm. She had a certain sweet simplicity and an innate shyness which was attractive, but Shelagh found it impossible to relate to her as daughter to mother.

That week of *Nagmaal* on the de Beers' farm became a blur to Shelagh. She did not understand the religious service, and few of the Boers understood English. The men were mostly bearded and taciturn, the women austerely dressed and suspicious of Shelagh and her father. She sensed, too, that he and she were disapproved of; a disapproval which extended to Maria, presumably because she was marrying a foreigner.

The marriage ceremony between Jack Maybury and the widow was completely without any attendant festivity. Indeed, it was almost a sullenly conducted affair, with the Boer neighbours looking on, grim-faced.

Afterwards, the wedded couple tarried only to consult a notary from Hopetown who was present, presumably to tie up some legal formalities, before the newly created family party returned to Mooifontein.

Shelagh looked at the children, who shared the back of the wagon with her, and thought dully—

My brothers and my sister . . .

Aware that she ought to make some effort to establish a relationship, she said aloud, 'Will you be pleased to return to Mooifontein?'

Three pairs of stolid eyes regarded her. Dirkie nudged Hannes, who nudged his brother in return. Rina sucked her thumb.

'Yes, miss,' Hannes said at last, acting as spokesman.

'You must not call me "miss", Hannes.'

'No, miss.'

Sighing, Shelagh abandoned the effort. Her father was driving the wagon, Maria seated beside him in a proprietary attitude. *Her mother . . .*

Shelagh shook her head. She had been on Mooifontein for almost nine months now, and she felt no closer to either Maria or the children. She doubted whether she would ever feel close to them.

After their return to Mooifontein Jack Maybury's physical condition began to deteriorate dramatically. It was as if he had been using all the energy left to him to keep him going until he had secured Maria as his wife and Shelagh's mother. Now it had been done, and his life-force had been used up.

He began to stay in bed. Shelagh was not even able to nurse him, for Maria claimed that right. She hovered over him, a now obese figure in her shapeless voluminous petticoats, or hurried on swollen legs between kitchen and bedroom, trying to tempt his failing appetite with tasty morsels. Shelagh, locked in misery, was only dimly aware that the two boys, Dirkie and Hannes, were trying to cope single-handedly with the farm work. Rina was like a mute, elusive little shadow hovering in the wake of her mother or Shelagh.

When Jack Maybury's end came, Shelagh did not even have the chance to bid him farewell, for he died during the night in his wife's arms. The next morning Maria sent Hannes to a neighbouring farm in the pony-cart, and shortly afterwards Boers began to arrive on Mooifontein, rigidly determined to pay their last respects to a stranger whom they hadn't liked or approved of.

The funeral service was made the more harrowing for Shelagh because she could not understand it. These people with their unknown tongue and their air of censure were in control of her father's laying to rest, leaving her no role to play.

No one lingered afterwards. They rejected Maria's diffident offer of coffee and rusks in the farmhouse, and left Mooifontein with the fastidious air of people physically shaking contaminating dust from their feet. In her grief, Shelagh hated them so much that she did not even wonder at their excessive and unremitting disapproval.

Maria touched her arm in a shy gesture, and quickly removed her hand again. 'Shall we—shall we walk back to the house together?'

Shelagh stared at her, pitying her in a dispassionate way. Maria's face had a greyish tinge today, and she held herself as if she were in physical discomfort. Shelagh tried to feel some warmth for her, and failed. She could feel nothing but personal grief and terror and despair.

'I'll stay here for a while longer,' she said.

'Try and cry, child,' Maria urged. 'You will feel better if you are able to cry.'

Shelagh nodded mutely, and turned back to her father's grave set within the alien and boundless veld.

Her gaze raked the horizon on all sides. There were no rivers or valleys, no wooded heights to vary the monotony of that hellish countryside with its endless vistas of scorching ridges and stunted scrub. And this was where her tomorrows lay. No love, no life, no hope. No father. No Luke . . .

She cried, then, harsh tearing sobs which tore her body and brought no relief. And when it was over, resolution had hardened inside her.

She would not accept the fate which stretched ahead of her. Anything—*anything* would be preferable to being buried alive on Mooifontein, waiting for life to tick slowly by until death claimed her. She would escape.

A plan began to occur to her as she walked back to the house. The next time the itinerant trader called on his way to the diggings, she would beg him to take her up with him. She would steal away from the house, and meet him somewhere on the veld. And when she reached the diggings . .

She shook her head. No, she would not allow herself to plan any further. Once she had reached the diggings, and Luke, she would let fate carry her where it would.

But Maria must not get wind of her schemes. Maria would stop her, and Maria now had the legal right to stop her. Shelagh would have to be very careful not to let her stepmother suspect what she had in mind.

Maria, however, seemed wholly engrossed in her grief and went to bed early. Shelagh sat on the *stoep* and watched Hannes and Dirkie drive the cows into the barn for the milking. Rina, as usual, hovered some distance away from her. The child had been crying; she had become very attached to Jack Maybury. Shelagh rose and went to her, compassion stabbing through her own numb grief, but Rina shrank away from her.

In the days that followed it seemed to Shelagh that the very walls of the little mud dwelling echoed the misery and grief enclosed within them. Maria made fitful attempts to return to her chores, and would be forced to retire to her room again. Clumsily, because household tasks were unfamiliar to her, Shelagh prepared meals of a sort in the kitchen, and dreamed of getting away from Mooifontein and this family of hers with whom she shared nothing more than the link of her father.

Exactly a week after Jack Maybury's funeral, Shelagh had fallen asleep when she was awakened by a low, almost animal, groan of pain. As she struggled out of bed the sound became a muffled scream. Frightened and puzzled, she sped towards Maria's bedroom, whence the sounds were coming.

By the light of a hastily-lit candle she saw that Maria's body was arched with pain, her hair wet with perspiration.

'What—what is the matter?' Shelagh faltered.

'My—my time.' Maria moistened her swollen

lips with her tongue. 'Three weeks too soon. Send Hannes—to fetch Lettie Botha.'

For a moment Shelagh stared stupidly at her, without comprehension. And then slowly the truth, which would long ago have been obvious to anyone less sheltered and innocent, began to dawn on her.

Now she understood the reason for Maria's apparently sudden gain in weight, and the reason for the Boers' disapproval both at the wedding and at the funeral. And her father hadn't told her, because he was trying to shield her from reality to the end, while Maria had been too shy to broach the subject.

Shelagh hurried, on legs which had started to shake, to rouse Hannes. Dirkie awakened too, and she told him to help his brother hitch the ponies to the cart. Then she sped back to Maria's room, in time to hear another muffled scream.

Some inherent female instinct warned Shelagh that Lettie Botha would arrive too late. She grabbed a corner of the sheet, and wiped Maria's face.

'What—what can I do? You must tell me.'

'Heat water,' Maria gasped. 'And tear up some clean sheets . . .'

The ensuing hours became a nightmare. Rina was awake by now, hovering near her mother's bedroom, until Shelagh told Dirkie, 'Take her into the parlour. Just this once you may play the harmonium.'

The children's eyes widened. The precious harmonium, no less than the parlour, was normally out of bounds to them. But they hurried to take advantage of this uniquely offered licence, and the laboured sounds they conjured from the harmonium served to deafen them to their mother's cries of pain.

The sky was lightening with the ghostly pallor of early dawn when Shelagh delivered Maria's baby girl. She worked by instinct now, for Maria was beyond telling her what to do and seemed to have lost consciousness.

The cord must be cut and tied, Maria had said earlier, explaining how it was done. With shaking hands and a mute prayer for guidance, Shelagh performed the necessary task. It was only when she had washed the screaming baby and was wrapping her in a clean sheet that Shelagh was able to stand aside from the panic, the desperation and the sense of her own inadequacy which had gripped her all night. As she gazed down at her puny half-sister she experienced the wonder of having assisted in a miracle.

She laid the baby down beside Maria, and prepared to give her attention to her stepmother. There was a blueness about Maria's mouth and a strange look in her eyes, as if she were staring at something which was visible only to her. And then she smiled, shuddered, and became still.

Shelagh stood rigid with shock. The baby's screams took on a desperate quality, as if she sensed that her mother had just departed this life. Shelagh moved then, picking up the infant and drawing up the sheet over Maria's face.

She walked slowly to the door. Dirkie and Rina had abandoned the harmonium and were hovering just outside their mother's bedroom. Shelagh looked at them, wondering numbly how she was to break the news to them. They seemed to sense tragedy, for they drew close to Shelagh as if by instinct.

From outside, the sound of hoof-beats reached them. 'That will be Hannes with Mrs Botha,' Shelagh told the children. 'Go and meet them.'

The Boer woman would know how and with what the baby should be fed. No doubt Lettie Botha's sense of duty would compel her to take the infant back with her, and various other neighbours would offer to take the older children in, splitting them up like a litter of puppies.

Involuntarily, Shelagh's arms tightened about the baby. Those stern-faced Boers would visit the sins of their parents on all the children; she had no doubt of that. They would take care of the children, but they would never let them forget that their mother had fallen from grace.

Indirectly because of her father, all the children were orphans tonight. He had left Shelagh a legacy of duty and she could not evade it. She would have to keep the children together, and save them from being cared for by some censorious, grim-faced *Boervrou.*

The trap was closing around her, the trap that would keep her on Mooifontein. Shelagh sighed, and turned her back for good on all those desperate plans for escape. She had begun to grow up. Luke would scarcely have recognised her now.

CHAPTER THREE

LETTIE BOTHA was a tall, heavily-built woman of middle years, with a dour expression and an air of command. Her eyes narrowed grimly when she saw that Shelagh was nursing the crying infant, for she realised by implication that all was not well with its mother. Without a word, she strode into Maria's room, closing the door behind her.

When she reappeared she looked at the three children, who had gathered about Shelagh. In an unfamiliar situation, they were instinctively clinging to her for reassurance.

'To bed with you!' Lettie Botha commanded.

Hannes shuffled his feet. 'I want to see Ma—,' he began.

'Well, you can't. Not tonight. Go on, off with you! I don't want you under my feet.'

The authority in her voice was such that the children left meekly. When they were out of earshot, Shelagh said, 'Thank you! I didn't know what to do, how to break it to them. But you're right; the morning will be soon enough—'

Mrs Botha interrupted her by taking the baby from her. She laid the infant on the kitchen table, and subjected it to a minute scrutiny.

With a satisfied grunt, she looked up. 'Did Maria make preparations for the child?'

'Not that I was ever aware of.'

'Well, she was bound to have kept Rina's baby things, at least. In the meantime, empty a dresser drawer and line it with pillows. And find me a clean blanket.'

Soon the baby was lying in her improvised bed. Packed away inside a yellow-wood chest in Maria's bedroom, Shelagh had found a stack of baby clothes, and the new arrival was bathed and dressed in garments which had once belonged to Rina. All that remained was to satisfy her hunger.

Fortunately, Lettie Botha had come prepared for all eventualities. In the carpet-bag she had brought with her was a feeding-bottle which looked as if it had done emergency duty for generations of Boer babies. This was soon filled with a mixture of boiled water, milk and honey. Mrs Botha showed Shelagh how to feed the baby without allowing her to swallow air, and went to attend to the laying-out of Maria.

With a strange mixture of feelings, Shelagh looked down at the baby in her arms. She was greedily sucking at the feeding bottle, a little rivulet of milky liquid running from the side of her mouth to her neck. How tiny she was, how vulnerable, how trusting . . .

Lettie Botha had finished attending to Maria's last needs. She came into the kitchen and set the coffee-pot to heat on the stove. Then she took the baby from Shelagh, and demonstrated how to change her napkin.

'Not that you'll have to concern yourself with such things for too long,' she remarked. 'After the funeral, we'll determine which families are willing to take in which child.'

'No!' Shelagh said sharply. 'I won't have them farmed out like puppies.'

'My dear girl, you can't reasonably expect any one family to take in all four of the children. To feed one extra mouth will be sacrifice enough for anyone.'

'I won't let any of them go. I'm planning to look after them myself.'

'And how, pray, will you do that? From what I've heard, your father left nothing, and if Maria had anything but the farm to leave, then it's news to me.'

'We'll live the way we did before Maria died. Everything she did in the past, I'll learn to do.'

'Have some sense, girl!' Lettie Botha rapped. 'You don't have the slightest notion what it means to work one of these farms! Maria coped because she was brought up to it. She knew how to drive a plough, how to reap and thresh and look after livestock. But even she would have been daunted by having to do all those things while also caring for a newborn baby. And you, a slip of a girl with soft white hands and not a muscle in your body—you imagine you could take over responsibility for a farm and four children?'

'I can't let them go,' Shelagh said helplessly. 'The baby is my sister. She belongs with me. And since she is also the sister of the other three, *they* belong equally. Can't you see that?'

'I see only that you are being very foolish and impractical. It's not even as if any of us would be able to help you with the work. Our farms are too scattered for that. Now, if you could have afforded to hire a couple of Griqua labourers . . . But Maria never could, so I don't see how you would be able to. No, child, what you are suggesting is madness.'

Shelagh settled the baby into her bed. She had fallen asleep, her closed eyes screwed up in an absurd expression of anxiety which went to Shelagh's heart and filled her with an aching tenderness.

She sat down at the table, and accepted a cup of coffee from Lettie Botha. Fatigue and reaction swept over her, and with it a daunting sense of her own inadequacy. How *could* she provide for the children—she, who knew nothing about anything?

Desperately grasping at straws, she asked, 'Is there anyone at all who could be approached for help? Just until I've learnt the ropes, and the baby is a little older? Do the children have any relatives—even distant ones?'

Mrs Botha considered. 'Maria's first husband was an orphan. His entire family was wiped out in a Matabele attack during the Great Trek. As for Maria herself, her father was an Englishman.'

'He was?' Shelagh echoed in surprise.

'His name was Henry Dixon, and he served in a cavalry regiment posted to Cape Town. He met and married Maria's mother against opposition from both sides. But soon after Maria was born he was killed during one of the Kaffir wars, and shortly thereafter his widow and the infant Mara joined the trek into the interior. On Maria's mother's side there are no living relatives. As for Henry Dixon—if he has any surviving family, I dare say they live in England, and will have no interest in the fate of the children.'

Shelagh said nothing. Weariness and tension washed over her, and she longed for the temporary relief of sleep. But she knew convention demanded that a wakeful vigil should be kept over anyone recently dead, and so she continued to sit by the kitchen table, and kept up a desultory, apathetic conversation with Lettie Botha.

If the children were split up, the Boer woman urged, the farm could be sold and each child's portion put aside for their later needs. And if Shelagh herself had no relatives or friends to go to, and she wished to stay in contact with the children, someone would offer her a home. She would be expected to earn her keep, of course, but she would be fairly and kindly treated . . .

In that wretched, melancholic hour before dawn, when the human spirit is at its lowest ebb, Lettie Botha's propositions began to seem reasonable and even attractive to Shelagh. Her resolution wavered. She had indeed been mad to imagine that she could keep the children and provide for them—

Mrs Botha scraped her chair back, interrupting Shelagh's thoughts. 'It's time to wake Hannes,' the woman said.

Shelagh's tired mind was still puzzling over the need to wake him so early when Mrs Botha returned to the kitchen, holding the bewildered, half-asleep Hannes by the arm.

'Is Ma—?' the boy began fearfully, memory returning to him.

'Jesus has called her home, Hannes,' Lettie Botha said. 'Go and kiss her for the last time, and then you must take the pony-cart and ride to Gert van Tonder's farm so that the coffin can be made without delay.'

'No,' Hannes began, his face working. *'No!'* His voice cracked with rage and pain and helpless bitterness. 'It isn't fair! Jesus already has our Pa and our stepfather! He didn't have to take Ma as well! *It isn't fair!*'

Shelagh ran to him, putting her arms about him. 'Oh Hannes, I'm so very, very sorry,' she whispered. 'Cry if you want to—'

He pushed her away, giving her a stony look. Then he walked blindly towards his mother's room.

When the door had closed behind him, Shelagh turned to Lettie Botha. 'How *could* you? I wish I had broken the news to the children myself, last night.'

'If they had been told last night, they would have been too distressed to sleep. And I needed Hannes to be fresh this morning. He has a long distance to travel.'

'But to tell him in such a hard, unfeeling way—' Shelagh began.

'Hard?' Mrs Botha echoed, with surprise in her voice. 'But life itself is hard, child, and merely a preparation for our entry into the next world. There is no point in cushioning the children against reality. It was God's will that Maria should be taken, and they must accept that.'

'It's too easy and convenient to blame everything on the will of God!' Shelagh cried fiercely. 'I didn't want to say this, but if all of you had not condemned Maria so implacably, she might have felt able to send for you earlier. Her life might have been saved.'

'What else should we have done but condemn her, pray? What she did was wicked and reprehensible, and her death bears the mark of divine retribution. Her death was ordained by God as a punishment for her sins, and when the children are old enough they must be made to understand that.'

Shelagh did not try to argue further with her. The Boer view was sincere but quite inflexible. And Lettie Botha had finally and conclusively shown Shelagh that she could not possibly abandon the children to the basically kind but utterly dogmatic control of the Boers. She didn't know how it was to be achieved, but somehow she meant to keep them all together and care for them.

When Hannes had left with the pony-cart, Shelagh forestalled Mrs Botha and woke the younger children herself, breaking the news of their mother's death as gently as she could. She held them while they cried, and then led them to their mother's room so that they could see her for the last time.

The day took on an unreal, frenzied blur. It seemed incredible that a mere twenty-four hours ago Shelagh's only concern had been to get away from Mooifontein. Now there was a baby to be cared for, the children to be comforted, and endless scratch meals and pots of coffee to be prepared for the neighbours who began to arrive in their ox-wagons.

While some of the men dug Maria's grave, others took charge of the farm chores. The Dominie, or ordained minister, arrived that evening. The burial was to take place the following morning.

As Shelagh tried fitfully to sleep that night, with the baby's improvised cot on the floor beside her, she wished that she could share the Boers' view which ascribed Maria's death solely to God's will. But she couldn't escape the thought that there might have been something she herself could have done to save her stepmother. If only she had known about the baby beforehand, so that she could have interpreted the warning signs correctly and sent for Lettie Botha on her own initiative . . .

She sighed, and turned over. Ironically, according to the other Boer women, Maria had for once done the correct thing in keeping Shelagh in ignorance. One did not discuss such matters with young unmarried girls. It was a terrible thought that Maria's excessive modesty might have caused her death, helped along by Shelagh's lack of observation and her absorption with her own unhappiness.

At the burial service the next day, the Dominie made much of the theory of divine retribution, and broodingly stressed the fact that Maria's baby had been conceived out of wedlock. Shelagh's tears were not only for poor, harshly-judged Maria, they were for her father, too, and for the loss of her own youth and freedom. They were also for Luke, whom she would never see again, and who was destined to become no more than a distant and barely remembered dream to her.

After the grave had been filled, the Dominie offered to baptise the baby. The name he favoured was Mara.

'A fitting name, for it means bitterness, and in bitterness was she brought forth.'

'No,' Shelagh said defiantly. 'I want her named Joy.'

The name—considered shockingly unsuitable—and her opposition to their Dominie, only strengthened the disapproval in which the Boers had held Shelagh since they learnt that she intended to care for the children herself. As they left Mooifontein after the service, many a head was shaken at her folly and stubbornness. She would rue it yet, they prophesied.

Indeed, almost as soon as she was left alone on Mooifontein with the children, Shelagh was seized by the enormity of what she had undertaken. When she had fed the baby and put her to bed, she called the other three children together.

'If I am to care for you, I shall need all the help you can give me,' she began.

'Why should you want to care for us, miss?' Hannes interrupted in a hard, unchildlike voice. 'You have never liked us.'

Shelagh flinched, but met his eyes. The child had a valid point. 'I was very unhappy, Hannes, and all I could think of was my own unhappiness. But now I have all of you to think of. When my father married your mother, it made us all a family. We're even more of a family now, because baby Joy is my sister as well as yours. And if we are to stay together as a family we must earn our living from the farm. I must learn to do all the things your mother did, and you will have to teach me. Tell me, as far as you remember, exactly what she did each day.'

'She rose at five every morning,' Hannes said. There was angry mockery in his voice. 'You wouldn't know that, miss, because you were always still asleep, and you were not at all interested in what any of us did.'

'I'm sorry,' Shelagh said humbly. 'Go on, Hannes. What did she do after she had risen?'

'She started the fire in the range and put the porridge on to cook. Then she did the milking, and gave us our breakfast. Afterwards Dirkie and I helped her with the field work while Rina cleaned the house, and fed the hens, and did the dairy work.'

Shelagh kept her eyes averted. Could all this frantic industry, this grinding labour, really have taken place about her while she remained oblivious to it, locked in her own misery? How appallingly selfish she had been . . .

She squared her shoulders. 'I should like you to teach me how to do the milking, Hannes. Until the baby is a little older I shan't be able to help you with the work in the fields. Could you and Dirkie possibly cope?'

'There isn't too much to do at present,' Hannes conceded grudgingly. 'Only the potatoes are ready for lifting. But later on, when the mealies have to be harvested and the land cleared and ploughed for next season, we'll need help.'

The baby began to cry then, and Shelagh hurried out to attend to her. As she returned to the kitchen she could hear the three children talking together. She had picked up sufficient Afrikaans to be able to understand the gist of what they were saying.

'We mustn't trust her, or get to like her.' It was Hannes's voice. 'She'll leave us. She'll never stay when she finds out how hard the work is.'

'Can't we like her even a *little*, Hannes?' Rina's voice was wistful.

'No! And you don't have to do what she says, either. She's not really our sister—'

'Yes, she is! Ma said she was.' At the mention of his mother, Dirkie began to weep softly.

'Stop crying,' Hannes said in a stony voice. 'Crying never helped anyone. Come on, Dirk, you and I have got to go and lift potatoes. We can't go on sitting around in the house. Ma wouldn't have wanted us to.'

By the time Shelagh entered the kitchen the two boys had left by the back door. Rina, tears coursing quietly down her cheeks, was rhythmically shaking between her hands a preserving-jar containing what looked like cream. Shelagh knew that the tears were for her mother, and sensed that an attempt at comfort on her part would not be welcomed. Instead, she asked with brisk curiosity, 'What are you doing?'

'M-making butter. The cream is still—what Ma separated . . .' Her mouth trembled.

'May I see what happens?' Shelagh tried to turn the child's thoughts. 'I've never watched butter being made before.'

In silence Rina held the jar towards Shelagh without ceasing to shake it. Small yellow globules formed in the cream, sticking to one another and growing larger. Rina stopped shaking the jar and poured the residual liquid into a jug, and began to wash and salt the butter. In an effort to reach the child, and give the illusion of a chore shared, Shelagh picked up the jug and tossed the liquid into the bucket of scraps destined for the pigs.

'Oh, what have you done?' Rina cried with angry dismay, looking up from her work. 'That was the buttermilk!'

'I'm sorry. I didn't know!'

'You don't know *anything*! You're the stupidest person I've ever met!' Rina began to cry in earnest—for her mother, for the loss of the buttermilk, for the comfort which Hannes had forbidden her to seek from Shelagh.

In the days that followed it seemed increasingly impossible to breach the children's defences. Shelagh's only consolation lay in the fact that the baby was thriving. In between caring for little Joy, she did as many of Maria's former chores as she could manage, and, even though it was not a fraction of what her stepmother used to take in her stride daily, she was in a state of torpid fatigue by the time she sought her bed at night.

When she thought of Luke now, it was with a dull, hopeless ache and not the rebellious passion of before. Her life had become a routine of grinding hard work and numb acceptance, and she knew that it would never end. It *could* never end. This was all life was to hold for her from now on.

When she did have a few minutes to spare, she sorted through Maria's personal possessions, deciding what to discard and what to keep for the children. Inside a carved box containing other documents she found a letter, dated just over nine years ago. It had been sent to Maria from England. It read:

Dear Madam,

Your communication addressed to my late father was passed on to me, as the present head of the family.

Whilst it is true that your father and mine were brothers, I must remind you that my Uncle Henry married against the wishes of his family. In the circumstances I cannot see that you and your children have any actual or moral claim upon us. I am naturally sorry to hear of your distressing circumstances, and if I were a rich man I would consider making you a charitable donation towards its relief. But I am not, alas, a rich man and so I must remain, dear Madam,

Yours regretfully,

Abel Dixon

Poor Maria, Shelagh thought, refolding the letter. How desperate she must have been to apply for help to her unknown English relatives. It must have been at the time when she was first widowed, and Rina was a baby, the two boys too small to be of any practical help.

It was strange and sad that only now that Maria was dead, Shelagh was aware of a sense of kinship with her. Like Maria, Shelagh had English relatives who would neither recognise her nor help her. And like Maria, Shelagh was struggling with the terrible responsibilities of a baby and a farm and dependent children.

Those same children were daily flinging tacit challenges at her, and waiting for her to admit defeat and leave them as Hannes had predicted.

All three of them watched her narrowly when Hannes announced one evening, 'We must start harvesting the mealies tomorrow, miss.'

'Oh yes?'

'We'll need Rina to help us. That means you'll have to do the dairy work, and see to the hens as well.'

'Very well,' Shelagh said wearily, wondering how she would fit in the extra chores.

'And when we've begun to stack the harvested mealies, you'll have to strip the dry leaves from the cobs in your spare time.'

What spare time? she thought dully.

A little defensively, Hannes added, 'It's what Ma used to do. We'll all have to work as fast as possible, so that we can do the winter ploughing before the frosts come.'

In that arid landscape with its grass always seared by the hot sun, autumn wrought few changes. Shelagh had scarcely noticed that winter was approaching. And next year, she thought, it would all begin again—the endless toiling, numbing drudgery.

With dismay, she watched the pile of harvested cobs grow beside the house until it appeared to her overwrought fancy to resemble a small mountain. Her days became a frantic treadmill. As soon as she had milked the cows, fed the hens and attended to baby Joy, she went to work on the mealies. With the baby deposited in the shade close by, Shelagh stripped the paper-dry leaves from the cobs.

The task was rendered the more laborious by the fact that nothing could be wasted. The mealie-leaves would provide kindling in that almost tree-less landscape, and had to be stuffed into burlap sacks for storing. Shelagh's hands became calloused, raw and bleeding, her mind a blank with the sheer unremitting monotony of her task. Throughout the day Hannes would arrive from the fields, the pony-cart stacked high with harvested cobs which he added to the pile as though he were throwing down a gauntlet. Only the knowledge that the children were working as hard as she was stopped Shelagh from becoming sorry for herself.

Even at nightfall there was no relief from toil. The harvested mealies had to be prepared for milling in Hopetown before winter came. After supper, when Joy had been put to bed, Shelagh and the three children sat in the kitchen and by the light of the oil-lamp threshed the mealies. Each cob had to be put singly through a small hand-winched machine which stripped the seeds from the husks. Again, the husks had to be collected and stored for winter fuel, while the mealie-seeds had to be sorted into bags. As they worked in silence, with the clock ticking away the seconds towards midnight and bedtime, Shelagh began to loathe the very sight of mealies.

'Hannes,' she broke the silence abruptly one night, 'couldn't we grow anything besides mealies?'

'We grow potatoes and pumpkins, miss.'

'Yes, I know. But something else besides.'

'What else *is* there, miss?'

She thought at first that the question was one of mocking insolence, and realised suddenly that Hannes, who had lived all his life on Mooifontein, simply did not know the possible extent of alternative cultivation.

'There's wheat,' he answered his own question, 'but that won't serve here.'

'There are also tomatoes and peas and beans and cabbages,' Shelagh said, and added with rising excitement, 'I'm sure *they* would answer. Mooifontein has a well which would provide all the water we'd need.' And the itinerant trader, she thought, would surely be able to supply them with seeds . . .

'Would suchlike things store for the winter, miss?' Hannes demanded.

'No, but we could grow them for our immediate use, and dry the peas and beans at least—'

'We've always grown just mealies and potatoes and pumpkins,' Hannes said flatly.

'Well, I don't see why we shouldn't experiment with other things too. When the *smous* calls again, I'll order some seeds, and I'll start a kitchen-garden next spring.'

Hannes made a sound of derision in the back of his throat, indicating that he hadn't the slightest expectation of Shelagh still being on Mooifontein next year. But Dirkie said eagerly, 'Could we have flowers too, miss? Ma once grew some flowers.

Blue, they were. Someone gave her the seeds.'

Shelagh smiled at him. She had become increasingly aware that Dirkie was an intelligent child, sensitive to beauty. 'I don't see why not—'

Rina, an ever practical soul, said scornfully, 'You can't eat flowers. Flowers are no use to anyone.'

'Some are,' Shelagh contradicted. 'Why don't we grow sunflowers? They are lovely to look at, and we could harvest the seeds for animal feed when the petals have died.'

Both Rina and Dirkie became enthusiastic at the prospect, but Hannes, who had been listening to the conversation with a jaundiced expression, obviously decided that his brother and sister were coming dangerously close to dropping the defences he had ordered them to erect against Shelagh.

In a loud voice, he changed the subject. 'What was that noise outside?'

'It's just the wind—' Shelagh began.

'It didn't sound like the wind to me. It sounded as if something had got in with the animals. Has the gate to the stockade been secured?'

'I don't know, Hannes—'

'You should know, miss.' His voice was hard and deliberate. '*You* were there last, when you drove the cows in after the milking.'

Shelagh was silent for a moment. Of course it was just the relentless wind which was making the animals restless. But Hannes had flung down yet another challenge, and she would have to accept it.

'I'll go and see.' She stood up, and lit a spare lantern.

There was something about the veld at night which filled her with a primeval, unreasoning dread. She guessed that Hannes sensed this, and that it was his sole motive for forcing her to go outside.

It was, she told herself, as if he had reached a stage where he was driven almost in spite of himself. He *had* to goad Shelagh into leaving Mooifontein and so prove himself right. She was beginning to believe that he would never drop his hostile barrier.

Steeling herself, she stepped outside and tried to shield the lamp-light from the tearing wind. Her skirts were whipped behind her by a savage gust, and she stifled a cry as something touched her ankles. But it was only some tumble weed rolling with the wind.

As she rounded the dry-stone wall of the stockade, the lamplight flickered in the wind and went out. The stars threw an eerie, unreal lambency over the landscape, providing just enough light to stoke her unreasoning fear of the veld by night. The vast, silent, brooding emptiness stretched out on all sides of her, making her feel at bay.

Something touched her from behind, and this time it was not tumble weed. Animal panic overwhelmed her. She dropped the useless lantern and began to scream, the sounds echoing off the empty plains and reverberating in her own ears.

She felt herself being spun around. Her terrified mind did not equate the hands which tried to confine her with a fellow human being. It was her enemy the veld she was fighting, and the hands were an evil manifestation conjured up by the inimical plains.

An uninvolved corner of her mind registered the fact that running footsteps were approaching, and that someone was shouting something above her own wild screams. She felt herself released so suddenly that she fell. The shock of physical pain stemmed her hysteria. Then Hannes's voice came to her from the darkness, fierce and unsteady.

'What have you done to my sister? Don't move—whoever you are. I have a gun. If you've hurt her I'll kill you!'

Shelagh struggled to her feet, confused, ashamed of her loss of control, and scarcely believing her own ears. Hannes had called her his sister, and was threatening violence on her behalf . . .

The next moment her heart soared with a boundless, incredulous joy. For Luke's voice answered from the darkness, curt with irritation.

'I haven't hurt her. If you really have a gun, then stop being an idiot and put it away.'

CHAPTER FOUR

ONE PART of Shelagh's mind remained detached and perfectly correct, so that she was able to reassure Hannes, introduce him to Luke, and explain that she had become foolishly panic-stricken in the dark. And while all this was going on, another part of her consciousness was exulting—*Luke is here! My love, whom I'd never thought to see again . . .*

'I hardly dreamt that you kept such dissolute hours on the farm,' Luke was saying drily. 'I assumed you would all be abed at this hour. So when I arrived I planned to stable my mules in the stockade without disturbing the household, and spend the night in the barn.'

'We were at work, *Mijnheer*,' Hannes explained stiffly.

'Were you indeed,' Luke returned in a thoughtful voice. 'You called Shelagh your sister?' He changed the subject.

'My father married Maria Steenkamp,' Shelagh answered him. Her first spontaneous joy was becoming blurred as reality encroached, and she was forced to face the fact that Luke had come too late.

It didn't matter why he had come. Even if a miracle had happened and he was no longer tied to a meaningless marriage, it would make no difference. She was committed to staying at Mooifontein with the children, her life dedicated to drudgery and duty, and nothing could change that bleak destiny.

Rebellion stirred fiercely inside her, and then flickered and died. It would have been better if he had stayed away.

'Let us go to the house,' she said, breaking the silence. 'I dare say you would like some refreshment.'

They picked their way in the darkness towards the homestead. The shaft of light showing through the open door of the kitchen forced Shelagh to see herself as Luke would shortly be seeing her. She had long ago packed away her fine gowns and had adapted Maria's serviceable clothes to fit herself. Tonight she was wearing a made-over dress of drab brown holland, streaked with dust and with mealie fibres. Her hair had been hastily and carelessly scraped back and twisted into a knot in her neck, from which it was escaping in untidy wisps.

Something—vanity, pride, a fierce refusal to be pitied—would not allow her to be seen by Luke looking dowdy, beaten and plain. She said abruptly, 'I think I hear the baby crying. Excuse me.'

She picked up her skirts and covered the distance to the kitchen door in a run. The two younger children sprang up when they saw her, their tense faces relaxing with relief, and she stayed for just long enough to reassure them that no harm had come to her.

'We have company,' she added breathlessly,

'and I must change my gown. I'm not fit to be seen in this.'

She hurried away to the bedroom which she shared with Joy. The baby did not stir when Shelagh lit a candle and opened the trunk in which she had packed away her stylish gowns. She had not expected to have occasion ever to wear them again.

In her haste, she slipped into the first garment which had come to hand. It was only when she fumbled with the fastenings that she realised the significance of her choice. It was the dark-rose foulard gown which she had worn on that fateful night in the diggings, the gown which Luke had ripped in his savage and deliberate display of passion. She had skilfully mended it, and she wondered if he would recognise it and remember.

She loosened her hair, brushed it and tied it back with a ribbon. Then, her colour high after her hasty exertions, she went back into the kitchen.

Luke had been talking to the children, but as Shelagh appeared in the doorway they all fell silent. She glanced obliquely at him through her lashes. The darkening of his eyes beneath their drooping lids, the small muscle which began to jerk at the side of his mouth, the involuntary clenching of his hands told her that he *did* remember. Something electric sparked in the air between them, so that even the children were aware of disturbing undercurrents to which they could not put words.

'Go to bed,' Shelagh told them. 'It's dreadfully late, and you're exhausted.'

The two younger ones nodded and went to the

door. But Hannes shifted from one foot to the other, eyeing her uncertainly.

'You too,' she urged. 'You and Dirkie will have to go out early again in the morning to continue harvesting the mealies.'

He glanced from her to Luke, and muttered dubiously, 'Would it be proper for you to be alone with the gentleman, Shelagh?'

The puritanical Boer streak, she thought with wry amusement, was already developing in Hannes. Then her eyes softened, for he had called her by her name for the first time, and he cared that what she did should be proper.

But it was Luke who quietly answered for her. 'You have my word, Hannes, that it will be entirely proper.'

Hannes accepted that, and left. When Shelagh turned back to Luke she saw that he was gazing at her with eyes which were blank now, and no longer held a trace of awareness.

'The children tell me that their mother and your father are both dead,' he began.

'Yes.'

'I'm sorry. She died in childbirth, I understand. But he—your father—was still quite young . . .'

'It was not unexpected. He had known for a long time that he was dying.'

'He *knew*,' Luke echoed grimly, 'and yet he risked saddling you with such a heavy burden of inherited responsibility?'

Shelagh sighed. 'He wasn't to know that Maria would die too. He did it for the best.'

Luke turned his head, and contemplated the

sacks of threshed mealies piled against the length of one wall, mute witnesses to the evening's labours. Then his glance shifted to Shelagh's scratched and calloused hands.

'Have the children no relatives who could help?' he demanded roughly.

'I believe there are second cousins in England. They don't acknowledge responsibility towards the children.' Shelagh changed the subject. 'I'll get you something to eat.'

'I've had supper, thank you.'

'Well, there's coffee on the range. It will still be hot. And later I'll make up a bed for you—'

'I'll sleep in the barn, if I may,' he interrupted. 'I don't wish to be too comfortable. I want to make an early start in the morning.'

She had grown still. Perversely, even though she had decided it would have been better if he hadn't come, the news that he was leaving again in the morning produced a sick roaring in her ears and a dryness in her mouth.

'Must you—' She swallowed. 'Must you go back to the diggings—so soon?

'I'm not going back to the diggings.' His voice was remote and impersonal. 'I'm leaving South Africa, returning to India.'

Overcome by a crippling sense of loss and despair, she moved to the kitchen range and pretended to busy herself with the coffee-pot so that he would not see her bereft expression.

'The river diggings are becoming too crowded,' she heard him go on. 'There was barely room for all the prospectors who had been swarming in, scrambling like demented ants along the river banks. And nothing of any great significance has been found lately. I decided to cut my losses and go back to India.'

Halfway across the world, Shelagh thought numbly. *I can't bear it . . .*

'Besides,' he continued, 'I haven't only been prospecting, but also testing a theory of my own. If one accepts that diamonds have been carried along in river-beds over millions of years—'

He stopped. For a moment neither of them spoke as Shelagh bent over the kitchen range, desperately trying to conquer the tears which stung her eyes. His silence made it clear that he was aware of her furtive weeping.

She heard him scrape his chair back as he rose. 'I'll go now. I shan't see you in the morning, Shelagh, so I'll say goodbye—'

She turned and looked at him through the blur of her tears. They moved together, and he put out his arms as if to receive her.

'Don't—sleep in the barn,' she muttered. 'Let me have something—something to remember in the grey years ahead . . . Let me have tonight.'

For a moment he was still. Then he took her by the shoulders and held her away from him. His eyes were shadowed with something like pain. But belying their sombre expression, the corners of his mouth lifted in a cynical smile.

'Time has taught you nothing, has it, Shelagh?' He fingered the lace *fichu* at her throat. 'The same gown, the same blatant approach. You really must cultivate a little discretion. One day you'll come up against a man with even fewer scruples than I.'

She shook her head blindly. 'It's no use pretending, Luke. It's no use trying to protect me from myself. I suppose you've decided that it would be wrong to complicate my life any further. But I know that you want me, that you planned to make me your mistress once—'

A spasm crossed his face. 'So your father told you . . .' His voice took on a harsh, grating note. 'Yes, I wanted to make you my mistress, but don't build any dreams on that, will you. You're young and beautiful, and I'm no saint. But your father whisked you out of my reach, and I put someone else in that role.'

'You—' She stared at him with sick disbelief. '*Someone else*—'

'Did you think you were unique?' His voice was brutal. 'I assure you, you were easily replaced.'

'I don't believe you,' she said numbly. 'You couldn't have come here tonight just to torment me. It must have been because you cared, because you wanted to see me for the last time, if only to say goodbye—'

'I came,' he said deliberately, 'because I didn't know your father had died. I thought he would have had enough of the rural life by now, and that he might be glad to share expenses with me in return for transport back to Cape Town.'

He turned away from her and went to the door. 'Don't waste any yearning memories on me, Shelagh. Some day someone may come along—someone in a position to marry you, and share responsibility for the children. It would be a shame if you were too blinded by silly dreams about me to recognise his worth. A futile shame, for we'll not meet again.'

For what was left of that night Shelagh lay face downwards on her bed, her body racked with soundless sobs of despair and disillusion and loss. Her life stretched ahead of her, stark and empty. How was it to be borne? How could any human being survive without hope, and with only bitter memories to fall back upon in the long, lonely, years to come?

She had just slipped into restless, dream-haunted sleep when Hannes came to wake her. It was time for the daily grind to begin.

In the grey light of dawn, Shelagh walked to the stockade where the milk cows were kept in a separate enclosure. Her heart gave a convulsive jerk when she realised that Luke had not, after all, made an early start. His wagon was drawn up beyond the stockade, his mules restlessly moving about inside. She opened the gate so that they could graze, and then she was forced to go into the barn to fetch the milking-stool.

Luke lay fast asleep in one corner, an arm flung across his face, looking vulnerable and defenceless. It was hard to believe that he was the same man who had trampled so brutally on her illusions last night. Shelagh swallowed, and moved noiselessly to where the milking-stool was kept, afraid of rousing him. It would be a pointless and painful anti-climax for them to meet again after the things which had been said. She would make certain that she was not around when he did finally leave Mooifontein.

After she had done the milking, and served the porridge which she had left on the range to cook, Shelagh addressed the children.

'I should like a change today. Rina can stay home and strip the mealies, while I help with the harvesting in her place.'

'What about Joy?' Hannes asked doubtfully. 'You couldn't trust Rina with her for the whole day.'

'No . . .' Shelagh considered. 'I could strap her to my back, the way I've seen the Griqua women carrying their babies. And we'll come home on the pony-cart when it's time for her feed.'

With the aid of a large towel, a sling was fashioned so that Joy could be carried on Shelagh's back. Fortunately the baby was adaptable, and accepted her unorthodox position quite serenely. Shelagh turned to Rina.

'Give Mr Valentine some breakfast when you see him. Tell him—' She stopped, and went on bleakly. 'No, it doesn't matter. There's no message.'

Shelagh found that she had underestimated the handicap which Joy would be to her in the fields. Griqua women habitually carried their babies on their backs while they worked, and made it appear easy. But to the uninitiated the unaccustomed burden seemed to grow heavier with each passing minute.

Shelagh trudged doggedly along the line of mealies, half bowed down by the weight of the baby strapped to her back. Her hair had come down and there was a streak of dried blood across one cheek, where a sharp mealie-stalk had caught her unawares and broken the skin.

Mindless with fatigue, she stretched up to wrench the dry mealie-cobs from the stalks and then stooped to drop them into the sack she was dragging behind her. Stretch, wrench, stoop, adjust the sling about her waist, drag at the sack which was growing increasingly heavy and cumbersome . . .

She paused in the laborious rhythm, her attention caught by a flash of sunlight on glass. Luke's wagon had drawn up at the outskirts of the mealie fields, and the reflected rays appeared to be coming from something like the lenses of a pair of binoculars. Her emotions blunted by fatigue, she registered the fact that he was taking a last look at Mooifontein before leaving it for ever, and mechanically she continued with her routine.

She was emptying her sack of mealies on to the back of the pony-cart later when Luke suddenly appeared from behind the surrounding screen of mealie rows.

Shelagh stared at him in dull surprise. 'You turned back . . .'

He nodded, and said tersely, 'I'll take over from you. Go home with the baby.'

'Take over . . .' she echoed stupidly. 'You're staying?'

'Only until the mealies have been harvested. If I help the boys, it should not take more than another three days or so.'

Shelagh bared her teeth in a bitter grimace. 'And

then the winter ploughing will have to be done. It goes on and on. It never stops—the work never stops. Keep your pity, Luke, and go to India and look for diamonds . . .'

He didn't answer. Instead, he called to Dirkie. 'Drive Shelagh and the baby home. I'm staying until the harvest has been gathered.'

By tacit agreement, Luke continued to sleep in the barn while he remained on Mooifontein. He took his meals in the house, and after supper helped with the threshing of the mealies. But there was a distant constraint between him and Shelagh, and neither of them made reference to the searing scene which had taken place between them on the night of his arrival.

His help made life easier for them, but there was no other comfort to be gained from his presence. Shelagh was ceaselessly reminded of the brutal things he had said, and she also knew that each day he spent on Mooifontein would only make his inevitable departure the more difficult to bear.

As they threshed mealies in the kitchen in the evenings, he enthralled Hannes, in particular, with his tales of diamond-prospecting in India and at the Orange River.

'What makes diamonds, *Mijnheer*?' the boy wanted to know.

'They're believed to have been formed by volcanic pressure, a combination of heat and temperature acting on carbon. They've always been found in river-beds, so that most people believe they can be found only in running water. But I don't. The same volcanic eruption which tossed the diamonds into rivers and streams must also have scattered them over waterless terrain, so that it should be possible to find them almost anywhere.'

'Do you mean, *Mijnheer*, that there might even be diamonds on Mooifontein?'

'I believe it's possible. If one could find matching traces of the volcanic rock in which diamonds are often embedded, or if one could find other minerals which are usually associated with the presence of diamonds, then I don't see any reason why diamonds shouldn't also be found. Here on Mooifontein, or anywhere else.'

The children stared at him with wide eyes. 'If we dug a very deep hole, *Mijnheer*, do you think we might find diamonds?'

Luke smiled. 'If I'm right, it shouldn't be necessary to dig a very deep hole. If I'm right, it should be possible to pick up diamonds on or near the surface.'

Rina slipped a hand shyly into the crook of his arm. 'Why don't you stay here with us, *Mijnheer*, and look for diamonds on Mooifontein instead of going all the way to India?'

Luke shook his head. 'I only used Mooifontein as an example, Rina. I said there might just as well be diamonds here as anywhere else in the world. I *know* there are diamonds in India, and that's why I'm going back.'

Shelagh looked up from her work. 'It's very important to you to find diamonds, isn't it?'

'Only as a means to an end.' Passion blazed in his eyes, and there was something ruthless about the set of his jaw. 'I made up my mind, a long time ago, that I would be rich. I'll make my fortune, no matter what I have to do—whether through diamonds or by any other means.'

Shelagh thought of the wife who had dishonoured him and the family who had disowned him, and guessed that his implacable ambition was connected with a desire to triumph over all of them. Even so, she felt a little chilled by his single-mindedness.

As she had predicted, immediately the harvest had been gathered in, the winter ploughing had to begin. Luke again postponed his departure and stayed on to help the boys. Shelagh could not understand why he should allow himself to be swayed by compassion, when they were nothing to him and he was bent on finding diamonds and a fortune in India. Each day, she braced herself for the announcement that he was finally leaving.

Instead it seemed to her that he threw himself with an excessive and uncharacteristic zeal into the farm work. Even after a day's ploughing had been finished he would walk out into the fields with a pickaxe and spade—to clear deep-seated boulders from the land, he explained.

In the meantime the children, and particularly Rina, were growing too dependent on Luke, and transferring the devotion they had felt for Jack Maybury to him.

'Why does *Mijnheer* have to sleep in the horrid cold barn?' Rina appealed to Shelagh one Sunday morning when he came in for his breakfast. 'Why can't he have Ma's bedroom?'

It was Hannes who answered her. 'It wouldn't be proper for *Mijnheer* to sleep in the house.'

'Why wouldn't it?'

'Because he and Shelagh are not married, and the neighbours would talk.'

'Then he and Shelagh must get married,' Rina said, pleased at having found the solution, 'before the frost comes and it gets really cold. Then they could *both* sleep in Ma's bedroom.'

Shelagh rose abruptly. 'Mr Valentine won't be here when the frost comes.'

Luke rose too. 'I want to talk to you,' he said shortly. 'Let's go for a walk.'

Shelagh hesitated. Somehow they had contrived never to be alone together for an instant since that first night. Then she shrugged.

Outside, a watery winter's sun turned the dew on the grass to a myriad sparkling diamonds. Very soon now that same dew would be transformed into frost. Luke *had* to leave before the frost came. The present situation could not go on . . .

'I want to buy Mooifontein,' he said abruptly.

Shelagh stopped, and stared at him. 'Is this a joke?'

'No.'

'Then you must be crazy. Why on earth should you want Mooifontein?'

He gazed into the distance. 'I've become interested in farming.'

'I don't believe you!'

He shrugged. 'Let us say that I've gradually become aware of Mooifontein's potential. You and the children can't hope to realise that potential. But

I can, with the help of a hired gang of Griqua labourers.'

'I still don't believe you,' Shelagh said flatly. 'You're no farmer. You haven't spent years in diamond-prospecting, testing all manner of theories, only to abandon it all and settle for tilling the soil instead! Why, less than a fortnight ago you were heading for India—'

'Damn it, does it matter what my motives are?' he interrupted irritably. 'I'm making you a straightforward proposition! This is no life for you—this back-breaking, gruelling, never-ending toil—'

'Why—why should you care?' she asked unevenly, her heart beginning to thud in her breast.

He glanced at her, and then away. 'I don't,' he denied in a flat voice. 'Don't delude yourself that this is an offer of disguised charity. I want Mooifontein. I'll pay eight hundred pounds for it.'

'Eight hundred . . .' Shelagh echoed faintly. 'You know perfectly well that it's not worth that.'

'I'll be the judge of that. I have friends in Cape Town who would help you to start a small school with the money. Your father saw to it that you had a good education, and you could use it to carve a career for yourself.'

'This is madness!' she protested. 'You can't possibly want to buy Mooifontein, except perhaps because you feel sorry for me and the children, and I don't want your pity—'

He made an exasperated sound. 'Very well, I'll spell it out to you! I told you once that I don't care *how* I make my fortune, so long as I *do* make it. And I've seen a way of making it right here on Mooifontein, instead of searching for elusive diamonds.'

'No one could possibly make a fortune from farming this land!'

'Not as dramatically or immediately as by finding a large diamond, no,' he conceded. 'But over a period of time, it's entirely possible. As I've said, I'd hire a gang of labourers and I'd grow things like cabbages, beans, onions, carrots. You know the kinds of prices the diggers are prepared to pay for such commodities. Half a sovereign for a single cabbage is not unusual. I would load my wagon each week during the season and sell the produce at the diggings.'

Shelagh was silent. It was true that the needs of the diggers could be exploited, and it was also true that a great deal of money could be made by supplying them with produce. But in spite of everything he had said, in spite of all his arguments, she could still not believe in his motives. She knew instinctively that he would always prefer the uncertainties and the excitement of diamond-prospecting to the surer but more sober business of growing vegetables for the diggers.

'You're no farmer, Luke,' she pointed out, 'and your heart simply wouldn't be in it.'

'Why the devil should that concern you?' he demanded roughly.

'I don't know, but it does. If you *really* felt there was a fortune to be made out of growing provisions for the diggers, why do you need to sink all your capital into buying Mooifontein? You could simply go on staying here, and I'd gladly give you a free hand to grow what you wished in exchange for a fair rent and perhaps a modest share in the profits—'

'God Almighty, woman!' he ground out, taking hold of her shoulders and shaking her roughly. 'I care nothing for you, but I *am* a normal, red-blooded man and you happen to be the only female on the place! I don't give a damn about your reputation, since you've already made it abundantly clear on several occasions that *you* don't care about it, but I do feel concerned about the children! I don't want them hurt by any scandal. So that is why I want you to sell Mooifontein to me, and get out of my life!'

She looked up at him, and caught an expression of torment in his eyes which was so swiftly concealed by his drooping lids that it might have been no more than an illusion. But she knew that it had been real.

He would probably never admit it, but his offer to buy the farm—and for far more money than it was worth—could have been made only because he *did* care about her. It was the only way he could think of to rescue her from the deadly trap of Mooifontein.

'Well?' he demanded. 'Will you sell the farm to me, Shelagh, and take the children to Cape Town?'

'It isn't mine to sell,' she told him. 'As far as I know it passed to the four children in equal shares when Maria died.'

'But you're their guardian. You could act for them.'

'Could I? I suppose you're right . . .'

'Well, *will* you sell the farm to me on the children's behalf?'

Shelagh thought of Cape Town, of civilisation, of an end to the drudgery on Mooifontein. 'I'd have to find out how the children themselves feel about it . . .'

'Let's go and find out now.' He began to lead the way back to the house.

Dirkie and Rina were enchanted at the notion of leaving the farm and going to Cape Town. But Hannes had doubts.

'Pa always said that land was important,' he argued. 'A Boer needs land.'

'What is the use of land if it takes every moment of every day to wrest a bare living from it?' Luke demanded. 'If Shelagh started a school in Cape Town she could save the profits and use it later to buy other land for you—land less inhospitable and grudging than Mooifontein!'

'I've heard it's good sheep country down Cape Town way,' Hannes mused. 'I've always fancied the notion of sheep-farming . . . Very well, I agree.'

'Good! That leaves only the legal formalities to be attended to.'

'When Papa married Maria,' Shelagh told Luke, 'I remember they consulted a notary who was present at the *Nagmaal* meeting. His name was Groenewald, and he was from Hopetown. I've no doubt that he holds the deeds to the farm. I'll write a letter, authorising the sale of Mooifontein to you on the children's behalf.'

Luke left for Hopetown the next morning, armed

with Shelagh's letter. She watched until the pony-cart was out of sight. Life would be easier for herself and the children in Cape Town, and she would be warmed in the lonely years to come by the knowledge that Luke had cared enough to sacrifice his ambitions for her sake. She would take what comfort she could from that.

Luke was still in Hopetown when a cloud of dust appeared on the horizon one afternoon, and soon resolved itself into the shape of a pony and trap. Their visitors were Lettie Botha and her husband.

Shelagh assumed that the Boer woman had called to see how the baby was progressing, and handed Joy to her.

'You seem to have coped reasonably well,' Mrs Botha said with grudging approval. 'I still feel you should have allowed the children to go to older, wiser, folk. There's a limit to what you can do by yourself, young woman. How, for instance, are you planning to withstand the forthcoming invasion?'

'Invasion?' Shelagh was astonished.

It was Mr Botha who answered her. 'That is what it will amount to. Some of us, I am sorry to say, will probably bow to Mammon and make what profit they can. Others are prepared to defend their land with shotguns, if necessary.'

'I don't understand—'

'Haven't you heard?' Mrs Botha cut in. 'A Griqua shepherd picked up a large stone, not far from here, and took it to Schalk van Niekerk—the same van Niekerk who sold the "Eureka" diamond to an Irishman for a few pounds. This time he showed more sense.'

'It was a *diamond*?' Shelagh asked in a dazed voice.

'It was,' Mr Botha affirmed. 'It sold for close on eleven thousand pounds. Mark my words, fortune-seekers will be streaming in, offering ridiculous prices for our farms—'

Shelagh no longer heard him. She felt as if every drop of blood was slowly draining from her body. With a muffled, incoherent excuse, she left the Bothas and hurried to the barn in a stumbling run.

It was not in the barn that she discovered what she had been looking for and praying that she would not find. It was in the back of Luke's wagon, hidden away inside a tin trunk—evidence enough to damn him.

There was a detailed sketch-map of Mooifontein, a thin black ink-line tracing what was described in Luke's handwriting as a possible buried watercourse. Crosses marked spots where his foot-notes stated that excavations should be made. And tied up in a linen bag was an assortment of stones which Shelagh recognised, from the time she had spent at the diamond-diggings, as quartz and jasper. She knew that, where these two minerals were found, there were very often diamonds.

She crouched on the back of the wagon, the damning sketch-map in her limp grasp, and remembered how Luke had often gone out alone with pickaxe and spade to clear boulders, as he had claimed.

He had known, almost from the beginning, that there was a very strong likelihood of diamonds being present on Mooifontein. That was why he had stayed. The diamonds had been his motive, and nothing else.

He had cheated her and the children, used them quite ruthlessly. At this very moment he was in Hopetown, transferring ownership of the farm to himself for a paltry eight hundred pounds, when it would soon be worth a fortune.

CHAPTER FIVE

FEELING SICK and betrayed, her mind in such chaos that she was scarcely aware of what she was doing, Shelagh returned to the house. Lettie Botha's raised eyebrows and expression of deep offence caused her to mutter something about having had to check urgently upon the condition of an ailing heifer.

Mr Botha cut impatiently through Shelagh's explanation. 'Have you given any thought to repelling the coming invaders?'

'No—'

'You'd better do so. Of course, the fortune-seekers won't be turning their attention to our farm, or to yours, yet awhile. It's Jagersfontein to which they'll be streaming, for it's out that way the diamond was found. They'll be pestering for digging rights, and if they're refused they'll start digging anyway, without regard for the Widow Visser's right of ownership. And when there are too many of them for Jagersfontein to hold, they'll spill over on to neighbouring farms.'

'Like a cancer on the landscape,' Lettie Botha put in grimly, 'they will deface our land with their corrugated iron shacks and their tents, and destroy our way of life for ever with their drinking saloons and their painted harlots and their godless ways.'

'We must be prepared,' her husband agreed. 'We must fix on a way of patrolling our boundaries, and stopping them from gaining a foothold on our land.'

It will be Luke's problem, Shelagh thought with numb bitterness.

Mr Botha was frowning. 'It won't be an easy matter. Our forefathers, the old *Trekboere*, staked out their farms simply by riding around an area of land. So if some foreign diamond-seeker stakes a claim to a piece of land and starts digging there, we couldn't do much about it while our boundaries are so ill defined.'

'Why,' Shelagh heard herself asking, 'don't you forestall them by staking claims of your own where you believe your boundaries to be, and dig for diamonds yourselves?'

Her neighbours stared at her as if she had taken leave of her senses. 'What would we want with diamonds?' Mr Botha demanded passionately. 'Can a piece of glittering stone compensate us for the loss of our freedom? Our fathers and grandfathers fought and bled for this land of ours! We have battled against drought and famine as well as against Griqua and Hottentot to create our farms out of the harsh bare veld. Are we to fall down before Mammon now, and dig up our fields to burrow for diamonds instead?'

Shelagh said nothing. She had scarcely paid attention to the impassioned speech. Would the children, she was wondering, ever forgive her when they grew older and realised that she had allowed them to be cheated out of a potential fortune in exchange for a niggardly eight hundred pounds?

Suddenly, anger broke through her other emotions. She would not take Luke's treachery lying down! She must at least try to do something about the matter.

The fact that he had not yet returned from Hopetown after all this time must mean that red tape was delaying the transfer of Mooifontein to his name. If she hurried to the town, she might still be able to prevent the deal from being finalised.

She said urgently, 'Mrs Botha, could you possibly take charge of the baby for me for a few days? The older children are sensible enough to fend for themselves for such a short while. I must go to Hopetown without delay.'

'Whatever for?' The Bothas were staring at Shelagh, scandalised. 'What could you possibly want there? And besides, you couldn't travel to Hopetown by yourself, a young girl like you!'

'I shall have to.' Shelagh hesitated—the truth would have taken too long to tell, and invited too many questions and profitless recriminations from her neighbours. Instead, she improvised. 'If we are soon to be in a state of siege against the diamond-seekers, then I must stock up with essential supplies.'

'The *smous* will be calling at our farms with supplies as usual,' Mr Botha pointed out.

Shelagh stifled an irritable exclamation. The devil take the Boers with their ponderous objections, she thought angrily. Struggling to inject a note of reasoned logic into her voice, she said, 'Just consider for an instant. The next time the *smous* sets out from Hopetown, he will be far more likely to bring with him equipment and supplies for the would-be diamond-diggers than new shares for our ploughs, or seeds for the spring sowing.'

'*Swernoot!*' Mr Botha was sufficiently aroused to swear mildly. He turned to his wife. 'The child is right! You can depend on it—the next time the *smous* loads up his wagon it will be with a view to making a killing from the diamond-hunters!'

'So you'll take the baby to stay with you?' Shelagh began on a note of relief.

'No.' Mr Botha shook his head. 'I'll accompany you to Hopetown myself, and lay in supplies of my own. Lettie can stay here with the children; our boys are quite grown up enough to cope on their own. Hannes can ride out with a message for them. How soon will you be ready to leave, Miss Maybury?'

'Just give me time to pack some food for the journey, and speak to the children,' Shelagh said.

The three children were less than enchanted at the prospect of being left in the charge of the strict and unbending Lettie Botha.

'Why do you have to go to Hopetown anyway?' Hannes demanded mutinously.

Shelagh bit her lip. While there was even a vestige of a chance that she might save Mooifontein for them, she did not want the children to learn of Luke's perfidy. They had grown to admire and trust him; it would be too devastating if all their illusions were suddenly to be shattered. But at the same time, she could not fob them off with the same excuse which she had used with the Bothas, for the children knew that they would not be here to need supplies.

It was Rina who came to her rescue. 'I expect,' the child told her brothers, 'that Shelagh wants to buy going-away things in Hopetown.'

'That's right,' Shelagh confirmed gratefully. She hesitated. 'But the Bothas don't know that. They think I'm going to buy supplies for the farm. It's best that they shouldn't know about—about Mr Valentine buying Mooifontein. They'd prose on and on about the land being your heritage.'

Hannes nodded and grinned. 'And they're sure to say that Cape Town is a sinful place, and that we shouldn't go to live there.'

Shelagh kissed them, and went round to the side of the house where her neighbour was waiting for her. Luke's mules had been hitched to the farm wagon; Mr Botha took up the reins, and then the rolling sound of the wheels as they passed over stone and scrub formed a heavy rhythm with the hoof-beats of the mules.

Mr Botha was a withdrawn and taciturn travelling-companion, leaving Shelagh more than sufficient opportunity to dwell upon her own painful thoughts.

'*I made up my mind, a long time ago*,' Luke had said, '*that I would be rich, no matter what I have to do*.'

And that, it seemed now, included cheating four children. It included exploiting the love which he knew Shelagh had for him, subtly allowing her to believe that he stayed on to help on Mooifontein because he felt something for her in return. When all the time he had been secretly prospecting for diamonds and plotting to acquire the land as soon as he found definite evidence of those diamonds . . .

She strove to give her thoughts a different turn, staring around her at the monotonous veld, its bare endlessness like a picture painted in sepia. There was no beauty or shade or softening patch of green to be seen anywhere. It struck her suddenly that there was a kind of magnificence about the stark plains with their occasional skeletal thorn-trees marking the few watercourses; something uncompromising, proud and cruel.

For the first time she had some understanding of the way in which people like the Bothas regarded this land of theirs. Like some mysterious, enigmatic and slumbering giant, the veld suffered those who made their living from it, but forced them to bend to its dictates, to accept its grudging, occasional bounty and to come to terms with its frequent savagery. And now strangers were coming; invaders who planned to ravish the giant and plunder the treasures which it hugged to itself . . .

She thrust the fanciful thought aside, and concentrated on forming some plan of action in the event that she should reach Hopetown too late. She would not scruple to fight Luke's treachery with treachery of her own. She was quite prepared to swear that her signature had been forged on that note of authority she had given him.

Long before they reached Hopetown the following afternoon, they began to meet the first of the adventurers swarming towards the new diamond rush. Their covered wagons creaked across the veld with grim purpose; they whipped their oxen along in a ferment of hope and greed as they hastened to where the latest diamond had been picked up. Mr Botha's expression grew more austere than usual, but he made no comment.

When they arrived in Hopetown they found another large influx of fortune-hunters seething in its street, stocking up with supplies and equipment. The town, which had formerly been no more than a huddle of shacks set along a wide, dusty track, had mushroomed since the first discovery of diamonds on the banks of the Orange River, and now boasted one or two stores and a hotel, as well as a modest church.

Mr Botha stopped the wagon outside the church, and turned to Shelagh. 'The Dominie and his wife will accommodate us in the manse overnight, Miss Maybury. I'll leave you with them now, and drive direct to the store. If you'll tell me what provisions you require, we can have the wagon loaded up ready to leave by early morning.'

She stiffened at this attempt to organise her time. She had no intention, either, of staying at the manse, for she had not forgotten the bigoted, unforgiving funeral service the Dominie had held for Maria.

Evasively, she said, 'I want to consult the notary, Mr Groenewald, about—about some property my father owned in Australia. I dare say he and his wife will offer to put me up.'

And if they don't, she vowed to herself, I shall sleep in the wagon rather than go to the manse and seek hospitality from your narrow-minded Dominie.

She reached for her carpet-bag quickly, forestalling any arguments from Mr Botha. 'I'll hand my order in at the store later, and meet you there in the morning.'

It was not difficult, in that small town with its one wide street, to locate the notary's office. Shelagh had to force her way through knots of people talking excitedly together, and the topic was always the same—the staggering news that a diamond of more than eighty-three carats had been picked up in the district.

Her gaze scanned the crowds bleakly for a sign of Luke. She would prefer not to run into him until she had seen the notary, and knew how matters stood. Perhaps, she told herself, the legal formalities had been completed, and Mooifontein was already irrevocably his. Perhaps he was merely kicking his heels in Hopetown while he awaited delivery of mining equipment from the railhead.

The thought impelled her to force her way through the crowd with renewed urgency towards the notary's office. She had her story prepared by the time she was seated at the other side of his desk.

'Mr Groenewald,' she began, 'I understand that a Mr Luke Valentine has consulted you about buying Mooifontein for the sum of eight hundred pounds.'

'Indeed he has. It was a week or so ago.'

Shelagh took a deep breath as she prepared to

perjure herself. 'I have to tell you that the authority which he presented to you was not valid—'

'It certainly was not, Miss Maybury, and so I made clear to him.'

'Oh . . .' Tension drained from her, leaving her deflated and utterly confused. 'You—made it clear to him? You realised that my—that my signature on the note of authority was—'

'Not worth the paper it was written on,' Mr Groenewald finished for her. He placed his finger-tips together, and leant forward over the desk. 'You signed that note in what you believed to be your capacity as the guardian of your stepbrothers and your stepsister. But you are not their guardian, Miss Maybury.'

'*Not*—? But there is no one else—'

'I'm afraid there is.' A look of disapproval crossed his face. 'Years ago, when Maria Steen-kamp was first widowed, and fearing for the fate of her children if anything should happen to her, she appointed a man named Abel Dixon, of Surrey in England, as her children's guardian. He, it appears, is their next-of-kin.'

'But Abel Dixon wanted nothing to do with her or her children,' Shelagh began, remembering that letter she had found among Maria's possessions.

Mr Groenewald nodded. 'I know that, and Maria knew it. But she argued that if she legally appointed him their guardian, he would be morally con-strained to stir himself on their behalf. I warned Maria that she could not force him to accept re-sponsibility for the children, and that she was prob-ably creating unforeseen complications for the future, but she wouldn't listen. Of course, when she married your father—'

He spread his hands. 'In the ordinary way, if she had died before her second husband, *he* would automatically have become their legal guardian and that other appointment would have been null and void. But your father died before she did, and so the position remains unchanged. Abel Dixon is the only one who can act on the children's behalf in legal matters.'

Shelagh bit her lip. 'Does Mr Dixon know that he is the children's guardian?'

'Oh yes. He also knows that Maria is dead. But he ignored all my letters on the subject, even though I have proof that they were delivered to him. He is obviously unwilling to be involved with the children. But it doesn't alter the fact that only *he* could authorise the sale of Mooifontein on their behalf.'

'And you told Mr Valentine all this?'

'I did.'

'What was his reaction?'

The notary shrugged. 'He accepted it, and said he would have to look elsewhere for an investment for his capital.'

Shelagh had listened with a frown. Luke, she felt sure, would not have given up as easily as that. 'Where is he now?' she asked.

'I don't know. However, he left a letter for you. He asked me to send it via the *smous*, the next time that gentleman set out for the Mooifontein area.' Mr Groenewald searched through a drawer in his desk, and handed Shelagh a sealed note.

She felt as if she had been struck in the midriff as she read the lying letter with its false note of sincerity. Luke had written,

My dear Shelagh,
I found awaiting me in Hopetown an urgent message informing me that my father is ill and wishes to see me. I must leave for England immediately. I plan to travel by mail coach to the railhead tomorrow, and then on to Cape Town where I'll take ship. So our transaction will have to wait awhile, but be assured that that school of your own, and the whole new life for yourself and the children, will yet be a reality.

Yours,
Luke Valentine.

She refolded the note slowly, with unsteady fingers, and kept her face averted so that the notary would not see her expression. Luke had hurried to England for one reason only—so that he could wring from Abel Dixon the authority to buy Mooifontein for a song.

It was easy to see why he had decided to go in person, rather than to rely on letters. Abel Dixon had already shown himself to be unwilling to answer letters which concerned the affairs of the children. In all probability he felt that if he committed himself to writing he would be tacitly accepting that he had some responsibility for them. Or perhaps he simply destroyed, unread, all letters from South Africa.

Shelagh muttered something about not taking up

more of the notary's time, and made to rise. But Mr Groenewald said, 'While you're here, Miss Maybury, I'll give you copies of the marriage settlement between your father and Maria, and also of their respective wills. I had been meaning to take them to Mooifontein, but pressure of business . . . However, if you would like to look at them now, I could explain anything that isn't clear to you.'

Blindly, Shelagh reached for the sheaf of documents which he was holding out to her. 'I'm—sure they'll be quite straightforward,' she muttered, and slipped them into her carpet-bag. 'I—I really must go now.'

Outside, she found that the sun was nudging the horizon, bathing the ugly little town in a flamboyant roseate light. Despite the new evidence she had of Luke's duplicity, she felt curiously bereft and desolate now that there was no fear of bumping into him.

Bleakly, she thought that he would have no difficulty in persuading Abel Dixon to sell Mooifontein to him. He would tell the children's reluctant guardian about Shelagh, and how she would use the proceeds of the sale to start a school and provide for her step-brothers and sisters. And Mr Dixon would jump at the chance of severing all links between himself and his unwanted young relatives in South Africa.

Shelagh considered writing to the man, putting the true facts of the case to him and pleading with him on the children's behalf. But even if he read the letter, it would inevitably reach England long after Luke had done so. No, it was only a matter of time before Luke acquired ownership of Mooifontein, and there was nothing she could do about it.

Life, meanwhile, would have to continue; she and the children would need basic supplies to see them through the winter, and it would be foolish to rely on the *smous* now that he had so many other potential customers.

Reflecting on the irony of it, Shelagh entered the supply store to order the very provisions which she had used as an excuse to the Bothas for her visit. She smiled dourly when the store-owner reminded her that she had committed herself, through the *smous*, to a special order of vegetable seeds. It seemed a long time ago that she and the children had planned to grow peas and beans and sunflowers on Mooifontein.

Shelagh supervised the packing of her provisions on the wagon which Mr Botha had left in the yard of the store, and it was quite late when this had been completed. For the first time, she remembered that she had declined to spend the night at the manse, and that even if Mr Groenewald had intended to invite her to stay with him and his wife, she had given him no opportunity to do so.

She realised now that her resolution to sleep on the wagon if necessary was impracticable. The store-owner's two vicious guard-dogs would be let loose to prowl the yard against thieves, and the slightest unguarded movement from Shelagh would send them leaping on to the wagon with savage intent.

She stared pensively at the hotel with its veranda lights winking invitingly through the darkness. The

Bothas would be scandalised, of course, but there was no need for them to know that she had put up at the hostelry. She had eaten the remains of a mutton-pie which had been left on the wagon, so would require no supper, and a room alone would not cost so very much. Resolutely, she set her footsteps towards the hotel.

Its owner, a kindly, avuncular man, spread his hands apologetically after he had listened to Shelagh's request for a room. 'It's too bad, miss! I'm sorry. Every room has been taken. Diamond-seekers, you know; prospectors and geologists and the like. Don't you have friends in the town?'

'No.' She stared at him in dismay. It would be too galling to have to knock up the manse after all, at this late hour, and attempt to answer all the curious, censorious questions which would be fired at her.

The hotel-owner snapped his fingers. 'I've thought of something, miss! One of the guests reserved an extra room; he said it was for a friend he was expecting. But no friend has turned up yet, and I doubt if he will at this hour, so I'll ask the gentleman to let you have the room for the night.' He had begun to move away as he spoke, but suddenly stopped. 'On second thoughts, miss, you'd best come with me. He'd find it harder to refuse you to your face.'

Shelagh picked up her carpet-bag and followed him along a veranda with rooms leading off it. The hotelier stopped outside one of the doors and said, 'I've had a better idea, miss. This is the room that's awaiting the friend. Go in and unpack your bag, while I go and speak to the gentleman who is paying for the room. He's less likely to refuse if you are already in occupation.' With a conspiratorial wink, the proprietor unlocked the door and stood aside for Shelagh to enter.

'*Get the hell out of here*,' a voice growled as she closed the door behind her.

She whirled round. The room was illuminated only by a dim light streaming through the window from the veranda. It showed her a man's figure seated on the bed, his head in his hands, a bottle and a glass on the table beside the bed. His slumped figure was as familiar to her as his voice had been.

'This—it can't be—' she muttered with dazed disbelief.

He lifted his head slowly. In that dim light Luke's face looked gaunt and unfamiliar, with long, bitter lines etched beside his mouth. He stared at her for a long moment before he lurched to his feet. His mouth was smiling as he came towards her, but his eyes held a stark, terrible expression, as if he dwelt in some private hell in which Shelagh's sudden appearance was no more than a temporary distraction.

'Well, well,' he jeered. 'So you tracked me down . . . Clever Shelagh—but as unsubtle as ever . . .'

She began to back away, and half-turned to the door. But his hand shot out, and he drew her against him.

'Luke, no!' Shelagh cried. 'I didn't expect you—I understand nothing, except that you're drunk—'

'Not so drunk—that I don't know—what you've

come for. I'm damned—if I'll save you from yourself again. I'm not made of stone—and I'm just drunk enough to stop playing the gentleman. This time—I'm taking what you've offered so persistently before, ever since we first met . . .'

She made a frightened sound. He cut it off by invading her mouth with a raw intensity which held far more than mere passion. She struggled with him; still struggling they landed together on the bed. She was pinned down by his weight, and his hands wrenched at the fastenings of her bodice while his mouth sought hers again.

She tangled her hands in his hair and pulled as hard as she could, but he seemed impervious to pain. Moving her head violently from side to side she forced him to lift his mouth from hers for a second, and it was all she needed. Grabbing one of his hands which had been exploring her body, she sank her teeth into his wrist as hard as she could. This time he gave a grunt of pain, and the sight of the blood trickling down his arm seemed to shock him into sanity.

She hurled herself from the bed, and stood heaving with rage and humiliation and pent-up bitterness.

'You *animal*!' she panted at him. 'You unprincipled savage! How dared you! You were the very last person I expected to find here tonight! As far as I knew, you were on your way back to England, to cheat the children out of a diamond-bearing farm by persuading their guardian to sell it to you for a song!'

He sat down on the bed and sank his head in his

hands. When he looked up at her again his expression was so ravaged and haunted, so bereft of hope, that her anger melted away.

'Shelagh,' he said quietly, 'I'm sorry. If I was more than a little drunk, believe me, I'm sober now. It's obvious that you've been to see the notary. But what are you doing here, in this room?'

'The proprietor let me in, because I have nowhere else to stay the night, and he thought it was unoccupied. Why did you come back, Luke? Surely your conscience didn't prick you about cheating the children?'

He made a rough sound and reached for her, grabbing her hands in his. 'I love you, Shelagh. Do you really think I would cheat you, or anyone who belongs to you?'

She caught her breath. 'You—*love* me?'

'You must have known it, no matter how hard I tried to deny it.'

'You—have a strange way of showing it,' she said unsteadily, struggling to think coherently. 'You planned to buy Mooifontein, knowing there were diamonds—'

'I picked up a piece of quartz on Mooifontein,' he admitted tonelessly, 'and that told me there were almost certainly diamonds too. So I began to study the rock formations, and I did some digging, and I found pieces of jasper. Then I knew, beyond reasonable doubt, that there *were* diamonds on Mooifontein.'

'But you kept the knowledge to yourself—'

'I had to,' he said. 'Don't you think I *wanted* to tell you? But secrecy had to be absolute.'

'And I was not to be trusted?' she asked with an edge of bitterness and suspicion. 'Nothwithstanding the fact that the farm belongs to my half-brothers and sisters?'

'Look, Shelagh, even the merest hint on the diamond grapevine would have started a rush, a wild scramble. And remote as Mooifontein is, your Boer neighbours *do* sometimes visit to check the children's welfare.'

'I still don't see why I couldn't have been told. Do you think I would have betrayed your confidence?'

He sighed. 'No. But in order to discourage any visiting Boers, I had to have the place to myself. You see, the secret digging I had been doing was no longer enough. It became necessary to excavate on a larger scale. There was no way I could have done that without arousing curiosity and comment from you and the children. And how could one have expected the children to keep such an exciting secret? They were bound to let something slip when the trader called, or a neighbour paid a visit, and then the farm would have been over-run by diamond-prospectors. So there was only one possible thing I could do—I had to buy Mooifontein and get on with the necessary excavations in secret and solitude.'

'You offered eight hundred pounds, a fraction of its worth!' she accused.

'You protested that *that* was too much, remember?' he countered. 'If I had offered more, I might as well have shouted the truth from the rooftops. I had no intention of cheating you or the children out of anything, Shelagh. I meant to register the mineral rights in the joint names of you, myself, and the four children. We would have had equal shares in all diamonds found on Mooifontein.'

He shrugged tiredly. 'As you so rightly guessed, I intended to see Abel Dixon in England once I learnt that *he* was the children's guardian. I thought I had all the time in the world. But I hadn't reached the railhead yet when the news exploded that a diamond had been picked up casually not far from Mooifontein, and I knew it would not be long before every man jack who owned a pick and shovel was swarming over the farm.'

'So you came back,' Shelagh said softly, the last of her reservations crumbling.

'Yes.' He hesitated. 'I formed another plan, Shelagh. It seemed to me that since this Abel Dixon refuses to answer letters concerning the children, and is virtually unreachable, it should be possible for Mr Groenewald to apply for temporary powers to act in his stead—to a limited degree, anyway. So if you and I go to see the notary together, we could explain it to him.'

Shelagh frowned. 'I don't quite understand what you have in mind?'

'You're the children's guardian in all but name, and you could tell the notary that you want the mining rights in Mooifontein to be leased to me. Because if we delay in the hope of hearing from Abel Dixon, the farm will be over-run with illegal diggers and we'll be powerless to stop them.'

'I see. Yes, I'm sure Mr Groenewald would have to agree to such a reasonable request.'

'We'll go to see him in the morning, Shelagh.'

She hesitated. There were still so many unanswered questions—why he hadn't returned to Mooifontein after turning back to Hopetown; who was the friend for whom he had reserved a bedroom; why had he been sitting in that bedroom over a bottle of whisky in the dark . . .

He was watching her, and the look in his eyes this time was one of longing and regret. Without thinking, she turned to him, and laid her palms against his chest. She could feel the wild beating of his heart beneath her fingers.

His arms enclosed her and he pulled her down beside him on the bed so that their bodies moulded closely together. He fumbled awkwardly, with unsteady hands, at the frogged fastenings of her bodice which he had earlier tried to wrench apart. This time she helped him, smiling into his eyes with tender amusement. He caught his breath and then his mouth claimed hers, gently at first, as if to make up for his earlier brutality. But under the instinctive sensuality of her response, she could feel his passion mounting, and she moaned deep in her throat as his hands moved from the hollow of her waist to cup her breasts.

The door opened with shocking suddenness. Luke released her and Shelagh sat up, hastily fastening her bodice, and blinking stupidly at the young woman who was studying them by the light of a lantern.

Shelagh felt dazed and disorientated, as much by the girl's devastating beauty as by shocked surprise at the interruption. The intruder wore a silk *peignoir* of pale rose, which cast a faint reflection on her flawless, almost transparent, skin. Her hair, tumbling to her shoulders in exquisite disarray, was so pale that it reminded Shelagh of moonlight, and her blue eyes were regarding them with angry mockery.

'Well!' the young woman breathed. 'One scarcely knows what to say in the circumstances!'

Shelagh stared at Luke. His face was as set as if it were hewn from stone. She turned to the stranger, and heard her own voice sounding far away and unreal. 'You—you are—?'

'Diana Valentine, of course. Luke's wife.' She raised exquisitely arched eyebrows at Shelagh. 'Didn't he tell you that I had come to join him—that we've decided to make a fresh start?'

CHAPTER SIX

THROUGH A dull roaring in her ears, Shelagh heard the young woman go on, 'But like many reconciliations, this one is having its stormy moments . . .'

Luke said in a low growl, 'Be quiet, Diana. Leave us!'

She ignored the command, addressing herself to him this time. 'I can only assume that this little scene was staged on purpose, to turn the tables and make *me* jealous. Because you must have known, my darling, that I was bound to investigate after the hotelier came looking for you, and I learnt that he'd let a strange young woman into the room where you were nursing your jealous rage!'

She swung around, and regarded Shelagh with derisive contempt. 'But it seems she is not, after all, a strange young woman to *you*.'

With a blind instinct to escape from a situation which she could neither assimilate nor endure, Shelagh grabbed her carpet-bag and fled to the door. She heard Luke call out to her, and then there was the sound of the door being slammed with force, presumably by his wife, determined to have the matter out with him.

The sound of her own running footsteps on the

veranda floor echoed insistently in Shelagh's ears, beating a tattoo in her brain. *'Liar! Liar! Cheat and liar!'*

Now she was in Hopetown's wide street, her precipitate flight attracting attention among the few people, exclusively male, who were still abroad at that hour. Someone called out to her in a suggestive, lascivious voice; another man started to follow her. She could hear his rapid breathing, and suddenly felt his hand on her shoulder. She turned with the intention of hurling her carpet-bag at him, and at that moment saw Luke looming up in the starlight. His raised fist made an arc as he swung it at her molester with full force, and the man sprawled in the dust.

Ignoring him, stepping over the outstretched figure, Luke grabbed Shelagh's arm. 'Come back! You are not safe out here at this time of night—'

'Leave me—alone.' Her voice was muffled with pain. 'Just—leave me. Go back to your wife.'

He made a grating sound. 'Don't jump to conclusions, Shelagh! You know absolutely nothing about the matter!'

'I know—as much—as I need to know,' she said unevenly, and went on with a travesty of a smile—'But tell me, Luke, did you send for her, using the diamonds on Mooifontein as a lure?'

He swore under his breath. 'No, I did not! We met on the road between Hopetown and the railhead, just after I'd turned back. I had no notion that she even contemplated coming here. God knows why she did. I would have sworn that nothing could prise her away from her high Society life in London.'

'It seems—the thought of a reconciliation could.'

'There is no reconciliation,' he said tersely. 'For some reason it suits Diana to pretend that there is. She is telling all and sundry that we're making a fresh start. It isn't true. Why do you imagine I took a separate room at the hotel?'

'You reserved it for a friend—'

'The friend does not exist. Before I could stop her, Diana had asked the hotelier for a double room in both our names. So I reserved an extra room for myself, and the only way I could avoid a lot of unpleasant gossip and speculation was to pretend it was for a friend.'

Shelagh shook her head. 'You're very good at lying, Luke. But I'm slowly getting better at recognising your lies.'

He grabbed her shoulders in a hard, bruising hold, and she could see the angry glint of his eyes in the starlight. 'Believe what you like! Good God, I don't have to justify myself to you! I've told you the truth. If you won't accept it, I'm certainly not prepared to plead my case with you!' He released her, and went on with less force, 'Now come back to the hotel. You've nowhere else to go and you can't walk the street.'

'Are you offering to give up your room to me, Luke?'

'Yes, of course.'

She said, in a tightly controlled voice, 'Well, I won't trouble you. I'll get a bed at the manse.'

To the left of them, flanked by the church,

lamplight was still flickering in the windows of the manse. 'If you're sure—' Luke began.

'I am. Goodnight.'

She swung open the gate which led to both the church and the manse. Luke waited until she had reached the door of the manse before he turned away with a shrug.

Shelagh thought of the questions with which the Dominie and his wife and Mr Botha would bombard her, and turned instead to the church. As she had hoped, it was not locked.

Inside the unpretentious little church with its smell of raw new wood she was able to give way to the shock and pain and humiliation which had been tearing her apart. A while later, when she had no tears left to shed, she sat hunched upon the hard pew and forced herself to review the situation with harsh honesty, sparing herself nothing.

If Luke had given up his room to her, where would *he* have spent the night? Where, other than with the wife whom he said he didn't want, and with whom he said there was no reconciliation?

Whatever the truth was about that extra room, the fact remained that Luke had been at the hotel for almost a week now with Diana, even the pressing matter of Mooifontein's diamonds relegated to second place in his mind. And whichever way one looked at it, no wife—and certainly not a sophisticated beauty like Diana Valentine—would have followed her husband to a bleak and comfortless country unless she loved that husband. Luke had, therefore, lied when he told Shelagh's father that his marriage had been a sham from the beginning.

It was probably a tempestuous marriage, punctuated by passionate quarrels and equally passionate reconciliations.

Luke had been lying steadily ever since, about almost everything. Shelagh's mouth twisted bleakly as she recalled him saying, 'I love you. Do you really think I would cheat you, or anyone who belongs to you?'

He had said it with his wife only a few doors away. His wife, who inspired such strong feelings in him that a jealous quarrel with her could make him wear that ravaged, haunted look which had almost taken Shelagh's breath away. And of course, it had been the blackest lie of all, calculated to render her even more vulnerable than she already was, because he wanted her help in getting the mining rights to Mooifontein.

He would never get them, now. By the time he called at the manse in the morning so that he and Shelagh could see the notary together, she would be on her way back to Mooifontein with Mr Botha. And Luke would surely give up trying after that, and leave the district with Diana. Shelagh had no expectation of ever seeing him again.

Some time after midnight she succeeded in falling into an uneasy doze, stretched out upon the hard pew, and she woke again before dawn. By the time Mr Botha arrived at the trading-store Shelagh was waiting for him, and they left Hopetown just as the sun exploded over the horizon.

Even the short period of time which had elapsed since they last travelled that route had wrought changes. The veld was scarred with the tracks of countless wagons which had trundled from all directions towards the new source of diamonds, and patches of scrub had been blackened by the travellers' camp-fires. Some of the diamond-seekers had even spent their enforced halts in optimistic and desultory digging, so that random trenches showed like raw wounds through the grass. And everywhere along the route they either followed or overtook fortune-seekers, a higgledy-piggledy assortment of humanity from all walks of life, from all four corners of the earth, everyone united in the lust for diamonds.

The Bothas did not linger at Mooifontein, but as soon as their provisions had been loaded on their own wagon they departed for their farm. Now Shelagh had to face the necessary task of telling the children that there was to be no new life for them in Cape Town after all. She did not go into detail, but simply explained that Luke could not buy Mooifontein since Shelagh had no authority to sell it to him.

Rina shed a few tears but more, Shelagh suspected, at the news that Luke would not be coming back than at the collapse of their plans. Dirkie pointed out hopefully, '*Mijnheer* still has our pony-cart. He'll have to bring it back, won't he?'

Shelagh had forgotten about the pony-cart and, indeed, that Luke's possessions—including his wagon and mules—were still on Mooifontein. With a mixture of feelings, she agreed, 'Yes, I suppose he'll have to come back briefly.'

Hannes said matter-of-factly, 'Well, if we're not

leaving Mooifontein we should get ready to do some planting.'

Shelagh nodded, glad of the change of subject. 'I'm going to make a start on the kitchen-garden tomorrow.'

Work was an anodyne and she threw herself hard into it. While Rina looked after the baby, Shelagh and the boys turned over the virgin soil for a kitchen-garden and sowed carrots, cabbages, squashes, beans and peas. Daily she found herself scanning the horizon for a sign of Luke, but he did not come, and after a while she decided that he must have abandoned his possessions. With no fortune to be dug up from Mooifontein, and with the beautiful Diana by his side, he had no doubt decided to change his plans and his way of life and had departed for some metropolis more suited to her style. He had probably reasoned that his wagon and mules were more than a fair exchange for Mooifontein's pony and cart.

Shelagh tried not to think of Luke, but sometimes his image would rise unbidden to her mind, and then she felt shattered by the savage pain and the sense of loss which swept over her.

It was not until some weeks after her return from Hopetown that she remembered the documents which Mr Groenewald, the notary, had given her, and after lunch she sat down to look through them.

Maria's will contained no surprises. All her property and effects had been left to her husband, Shelagh's father, and in the event of his prior death it was to pass in equal shares to Hannes, Dirkie and Rina. No provision had been made for baby Joy, who had not been born when the will was drawn up.

Sadly, Shelagh reached for her father's will. It could be no more than a legal formality, for he had owned nothing beyond his personal effects, and his remittance had come to an end with his death. Then she stiffened with incredulity.

'Hannes,' she asked in an abrupt voice, 'how big is a *morgen* of land?'

'Not very big.'

'If you took this house as its nucleus, its centre, how far would a *morgen* extend all around it?'

He thought for a moment. 'It would take in the kitchen-garden on one side, the stockade, the corn-store, and then the well. It would finish up to include that clump of prickly-pear cactus where the ground dips down in a kind of hollow pan. Why?'

Shelagh hesitated. 'I just wondered,' she said at last.

Her discovery was too new, its significance too emotional, for her to want to share it with anyone at that moment, even the children. For at the time of his marriage, it transpired, her father had formally bought, at market value, a *morgen* of Mooifontein's land from Maria, with the farm-house at the heart of it. And this *morgen* of land he had bequeathed to Shelagh in his will.

Her eyes blurred with tears as she read the explanation for his action. It had been done so that she would never regard herself as being an inter-loper, living on charity, with no rights. It had also been done to protect her, should the three Steenkamp children one day try to push her out.

There were legal conditions to her inheritance.

She could never sell her small piece of land independently; it could only be sold to the three Steenkamp children jointly, and then for a nominal sum. Her patch of land therefore had no intrinsic value as such, but it gave her a legal and moral stake in Mooifontein. It also meant that the farm could never be sold without her consent and co-operation, since no one would want to buy a farm of which a *morgen* at its centre belonged to someone else.

Shelagh put the documents away, and asked Hannes to pace out for her the approximate perimeter of a *morgen* of land, extending in a circle from the house.

'Why do you want me to do this, Shelagh?' the boy asked, puzzled, as they went outside.

'I know it's foolish of me, and—well, I hope you'll understand, and not feel resentful—but this piece of land is legally mine, and I never thought I would have such a proud feeling of ownership.' She explained what her father had done, and when she had finished, Hannes said simply, 'I'm glad. You're our sister, and it's right that you should have a piece of Mooifontein. When I grow up I'm going to see to it that Joy has a share too.'

Choked by sudden emotion, unable to speak, Shelagh ruffled his hair and he grinned at her. 'Tell you what, while we're waiting to sow the mealies, I'll mark your boundary out for you with stones. Then you'll be able to see exactly how much of Mooifontein is yours.'

True to his word, he began to mark the boundary for her, and whenever she had a free moment

Shelagh contributed to the cairns of stone round her piece of land. This was not only an expression of pride of ownership, but it also gave her the comforting illusion of erecting a barricade against invaders. For they *were* faced with the danger of being invaded.

Hardly a day passed, now, but that some would-be diamond miner called at Mooifontein, requesting permission to dig there, and some of them became abusive when Shelagh refused. It would not be long, she sensed uneasily, before someone ignored her objections and began to dig willy-nilly.

One morning, not long after Hannes and Dirkie had set out to sow mealie-seeds in the bottom field, they returned to the house, breathless with excitement.

'Shelagh!' Dirkie cried. 'Guess what! *Mijnheer* is back!'

'*Mijnheer?*' Her heart began to beat thunderously in her breast. 'I suppose,' she said, trying to speak calmly, 'that he has come for his wagon and mules after all. Where is he? Rounding up the mules?'

'No,' Hannes said, frowning. 'He and a whole gang of Griqua men are busy putting up fences around Mooifontein's land.'

'What?' Shelagh's first swift and unreasoning joy turned to bewilderment and a sense of disquiet. 'Did he say why he was doing it?'

'He said I wasn't to worry about it, that it was to keep people out. And you know, Shelagh, it wouldn't be a bad thing if we *could* keep them out. I didn't like the look of that German who asked permission to dig yesterday.'

'All the same . . . What *right* does Luke have to come and enclose our land?' Her anger rising, she jumped to her feet. 'Rina, look after the baby, will you. I'm going to find out what this is all about.'

Luke saw her long before she reached the spot where he, in company with some dozen Griquas, was erecting a double barbed-wire fence around the perimeter of Mooifontein. He threw down his tools and came to meet her.

In spite of everything, her heart contracted at sight of him. But the Luke who towered over her and stared grimly down at her was subtly changed. The old look of cynical amusement in his eyes was no longer there. Instead, they wore a hard, relentless expression. There was no hint of softness, of vulnerability, about him at all. He might have been a stranger.

'Well, Shelagh?' he said, an umistakable challenge in his voice.

She drew a deep breath. 'What—what do you imagine you're doing, Luke?'

'Protecting my interests.'

'*Your* interests?'

'Certainly. I hold the mining rights to Mooifontein, and I have no intention of permitting any illegal diggers.'

Shelagh said angrily, 'Do you think I'm a fool? Of course you don't hold the mining rights! Mr Groenewald would never have helped you to obtain them without my agreement!'

'But he had your agreement,' Luke pointed out coolly. 'Both the notary and the Court accepted the original letter of authority which you gave me as evidence of your feelings in the matter. After all, you were agreeable to my buying Mooifontein, so why should you object to my leasing it instead?'

'You knew I would object!' Shelagh cried furiously. 'When I did not visit Mr Groenewald with you, you must have known that I'd changed my mind, that I wanted nothing further to do with you!'

'Yes, of course I knew,' he agreed with implacable calm. 'And that's why I went ahead on my own. The Court has authorised Mr Groenewald to act for the children until Abel Dixon, their guardian, can be persuaded to take over his responsibilities, and I have been leased the digging rights at a rental of twenty guineas a month.'

Shelagh was too outraged to speak for a moment. She heard him go on, with a hard note of mockery in his voice, 'My presence here need not disturb you unduly. I see that preparations have been made for planting the fields; well, that can go on. As you probably know, from the sketches I made, my interest lies chiefly in that shallow pan by the prickly-pear cactus. I'll be digging there, and camping on the site—'

'No, you won't!' she interrupted with vengeful pleasure. 'That piece of land belongs to *me*, Luke, and no Court in the world would give you the right to dig there without my consent!'

He was frowning. 'Mooifontein belongs to the three Steenkamp children—'

'All but a *morgen* extending around the farmhouse,' Shelagh corrected triumphantly. 'My father bought it from Maria, and willed it to me, and the pan where you believe the diamonds to be lies well within the *morgen*. I don't know why it hadn't occurred to me before. Perhaps it's because, unlike you, I'm not obsessed with greed for diamonds—'

He ignored the taunt, and gave her a long, hard look. 'May I see the evidence of your ownership?'

'Certainly you may.' She began to lead the way back to the house, and he fell into step beside her.

After a while she broke the silence in a carefully neutral voice. 'Is your wife still in Hopetown?'

'She is.' Luke's tone gave her no encouragement to pursue the subject, and she lapsed into silence again.

When they reached the cairns of stone, Shelagh pointed out the perimeter of her property. 'As you can see, there is no question whatsoever but that the spot where you want to dig is on my land.'

He did not respond, but his expression became more grimly uncompromising than before, and only softened briefly when Rina hurled herself at him in an excess of joy as they entered the house.

Shelagh asked the children to excuse them, and took Luke into the parlour, where she handed him her father's will. He read it carefully, without comment. At last he handed it back to her.

'It was,' he said, beginning to pace the floor, 'important to me before to excavate that pan, Shelagh. It's more important now than ever. Diana—'

He broke off, and abandoned whatever it was he had been about to say concerning his wife. 'I need money,' he went on tersely. 'A great deal of money. I'd offer you the eight hundred pounds which I was originally prepared to pay for Mooifontein, but most of that has gone—'

He stopped again, abruptly. Diana, Shelagh thought, must have extraordinarily expensive tastes if she had found it possible to spend eight hundred pounds in a small place like Hopetown in such a short time.

'I can't offer you money, Shelagh,' Luke went on. 'But if you were to write a note to Mr Groenewald, indicating that you wish to sell your *morgen* of land to the children for a nominal sum, I could take it to him and be back here within three days. My existing lease of the mining rights would then cover the whole of Mooifontein, and I could start excavating immediately. I would give you a one-third share in all diamonds I dug up—'

'No,' Shelagh said quietly.

He bit off an exclamation of frustration. 'Look, put aside your personal feelings about me, and consider my offer in a business-like manner! Perhaps you don't consider one-third sufficient.'

'No, it isn't that.'

'Then what *is* your objection?'

Shelagh was silent. She did not know, herself, just why she was so adamantly opposed to the thought of giving up any of her rights in her *morgen* of land. It was not merely because she could not tolerate the thought of Luke excavating a fortune in diamonds from her property and lavishing their proceeds on Diana. Nor was it entirely because her father had gone to such lengths to leave it to her, or a desire for revenge because Luke had behaved in such a perfidious manner over the mining rights. All of these reasons were partly bound up with the stand she was taking, and yet it went much deeper, and was rooted in a strong instinct that her piece of land should remain inviolate.

'I don't want to sell my *morgen* of land,' she tried to explain.

'Very well, then, come into partnership with me, and allow me to excavate.'

Shelagh shook her head, and said, 'Even if there *are* diamonds in that pan, Luke—which is by no means certain—they may be of industrial quality only, and worth hardly anything!'

'That is a gamble I'll have to take.'

'It's not a gamble *I'm* willing to take! I'm not having the place torn to pieces, perhaps for nothing. We've just put in vegetable seeds, too, for a kitchen-garden—'

'Good God!' Luke exploded. 'There may be a fortune in diamonds waiting to be dug up, and you're concerned with a few vegetable seeds!'

Shelagh looked at him, hating him for making her sound foolish and for failing to understand that the vegetable seeds were just one small part of her instinctive conviction that the children's security must come first. Couldn't he see that she couldn't afford to be carried away by visions of diamonds some time in the future, if they were lucky? She had to think of tomorrow. If it turned out that there were no diamonds of significance after all, they would be left with a wasteland. The holes which had been dug would become catchment areas when it rained, and cause further subsidence, and the house would be unsafe because of excavations which had taken place so close to it. Life would be much harder even than it had been before.

She said angrily, 'I don't have to explain my reasons to you, Luke! Why *should* I give in, when merely by refusing to let you mine my piece of land I could be rid of you for good?'

His expression altered as he gazed down at her, stripping away her defences, leaving her exposed and vulnerable. 'Do you *really* wish to be rid of me for good, Shelagh?' he asked softly.

She looked down, so that he would not see the sudden tears which had sprung to her eyes. 'I hate you, Luke,' she whispered fiercely.

'No, you don't.' He took her chin in his hand, and forced her head up. 'Do you?'

'Leave me alone! Go home to your wife, Luke!'

Something ferocious flickered in his eyes, and was gone. 'I'll leave, Shelagh, but I'll be back. I'm going to fight you, you know. Before I'm through you're going to beg me to mine that piece of land of yours!'

He gave her an ominous smile and left the house, and a while later she saw him hitching his mules to the wagon. A feeling of unease remained with her, and sharpened into something like panic the next morning when the Griqua labourers whom Luke had hired arrived with bales of barbed wire and began to enclose Shelagh's *morgen* of land on all sides.

Hannes, who could speak a few words of their language, argued with them, but they went stoically on with what they were doing. They were, they said, simply following instructions from Luke.

After lengthy negotiations between them and Hannes, and only on payment of a couple of laying hens, the Griquas agreed to leave a small gap in the fence, just large enough to allow the livestock to be driven through one by one. Apart from that small gap Shelagh and the children were virtually marooned inside a prison of barbed wire.

Tight-lipped with anger, Shelagh helped the boys to drive the cows laboriously out to graze. If they should need to use the trap, she reflected with fury, they would be obliged to take it apart and assemble it again on the other side of the fence.

'Couldn't we cut the wretched thing down?' she asked Hannes.

'We have nothing strong enough to cut through those wires. Don't worry, Shelagh. It must be a mistake. The Griquas misunderstood something *Mijnheer* said. As soon as he comes back, he'll have it put right.'

No, he won't, she thought grimly. It was no mistake. It was his first offensive in trying to force her to give in to his demands.

She was not prepared for his next one. He returned to Mooifontein with his wagon and mules, and Shelagh caught her breath with pain and incredulity when she saw that he had brought Diana with him. They did not come to the house; instead, Luke began to pitch a tent just beyond the barbed-wire fence and gave every appearance of settling in for a long stay.

Watching from the house, Shelagh saw that

Diana made no attempt to help as Luke carried their belongings from the wagon to the tent. His wife was dressed in a gown of some fragile rose-coloured material, and wore a frivolous bonnet more suited to a day at the races in England than to a stark, barren, South African veld.

It was easy to understand why Luke had brought his wife. Apart from wanting her by his side, he had known how unendurable Shelagh would find the sight of them together on her doorstep. What was more puzzling was the question of why someone like Diana had consented to leave the comparative comfort of the hotel in Hopetown for a nomadic life in a tent.

Shelagh forced herself to walk to the fence and address them. Diana was seated on a stool in the shade cast by the wagon, while Luke was building a fire. Diana gave her a dour smile.

'Luke insisted that you would be unwilling to put us up at your house. I suppose he was right?'

'I'm afraid so,' Shelagh said with stiff politeness. She turned to Luke. 'Will you please arrange for this absurd fence to be taken down immediately? Your lease gives you no right to encroach on our lives in this way!'

'Oh, but you mistake the matter,' he returned blandly. 'I'm interpreting the terms of my lease to the letter. I am empowered to dig anywhere on Mooifontein provided that I do not interfere with cultivated fields and do nothing to endanger live-stock. The fence is there to protect your livestock. You wouldn't wish them to fall into a trench I had excavated, would you?'

Shelagh gave him a look of impotent fury and walked away. During the following days Luke busied himself in digging trenches while Diana sat in the shade and read a journal. Shelagh tried to ignore them, tried not to think of them together inside that tent at night, and tried to carry on with daily life, made so much more difficult now because of that wretched fence.

A week after Luke and Diana had established themselves on Shelagh's threshold, Hannes came into the house to announce that a stranger had left his conveyance outside the barbed-wire fence and was walking to the house.

'Another miner wanting permission to dig,' Shelagh concluded with irritation.

But the young man who knocked on the door a short while later was scarcely typical of the adventurers and diamond-seekers who had come their way before.

Of medium height and slim build, he was so impeccably dressed that it was difficult to believe he had been travelling through the dusty veld. His hair was the colour of pale gold and his eyes were very blue and set between long, curling lashes. If he had been a woman, Shelagh thought, slightly dazed, he would have been a beauty.

He gave her a dazzling smile, and extended a slim white hand.

'I believe you must be Miss Maybury,' he said. 'My name is Abel Dixon, and I have come to take charge of the affairs of my young wards.'

CHAPTER SEVEN

SHELAGH IGNORED the young man's outstretched hand. She was staring at him with acute suspicion.

'You can't be,' she said flatly. 'You're not old enough.'

He laughed, unperturbed. 'I believe twenty-one to be the minimum age required of a guardian. I, my dear Miss Maybury, am twenty-six.' His glance went beyond her, to where the three Steenkamp children were hovering in the background, staring at him. 'Ah, my three wards, I presume! Come and shake hands with me, and tell me your names.'

The children remained stolidly unresponsive, awaiting their cue from Shelagh. She said, shortly, 'I meant that you're not old enough to be the Abel Dixon whom Maria Steenkamp appointed her children's guardian. She wrote to him more than nine years ago, when *you* would have been in your teens.'

The young man nodded. 'That letter was written to my father, who also bore the name Abel. If I may come inside, Miss Maybury, I shall gladly explain.'

She hesitated, and then said, 'Very well.'

He followed her into the parlour, and once again

the three children hovered warily in the doorway. 'Can you prove your identity?' Shelagh asked, still suspicious and on her guard.

In reply, the young man drew from his pocket several letters, all addressed to Abel Dixon Esq., in Woking, Surrey. One of the letters bore a South African postmark, and she recognised the handwriting of Mr Groenewald. On reflection, Shelagh realised that the visitor had known her name, and could have learnt it only from the notary's correspondence.

'I must explain first of all, Miss Maybury,' Dixon began, 'that I am not like my father. *He* was a cold, heartless man, as you would probably have guessed from his refusal to accept responsibility for the children.'

She said nothing, but waited for him to go on.

'I myself knew nothing of their existence. My father had never mentioned the fact that we had family connections in South Africa. He died six months ago and it was only when I went through his papers that I found the letters regarding the children.'

'Your father was appointed the children's guardian,' Shelagh broke in. 'That doesn't mean that *you* have any responsibility for them.'

His gaze rested earnestly upon her. 'I don't see it that way, Miss Maybury. I inherited my father's worldly possessions, and so I morally inherited his responsibilities as well.'

'That's a very generous view to take,' Shelagh said, 'but it doesn't make you their legal guardian, does it?'

'I *am* their legal guardian,' Abel Dixon confirmed. 'I consulted my lawyer before I left England. Even if I had not chosen to take over that role from my father, I am the children's next-of-kin, and therefore responsible for them.'

Shelagh glanced at the three children, who were still hovering in the doorway and regarding Abel Dixon as if he were a being from another planet. And then she studied the young man.

His clothes were of the finest cut and style, indicating that he had expensive tastes. He was also something of a fop. Why should someone like that wish to concern himself with three children whom he had never set eyes on before?

'I am not a wealthy man', his father had written to Maria when he rejected her appeal for help on the children's behalf. If that were true, then his legacy to his son could not have been a large one; certainly not large enough to give full scope to the young Abel Dixon's foppish tastes.

Those wide blue eyes of his, Shelagh thought, were a shade *too* artless and sincere. Would he have hastened to South Africa to claim responsibility for the children in person if the world were not still convulsed with the sensational news that a fabulous diamond had been found in the vicinity?

Aloud, she asked abruptly, 'Are you still living in your late father's house in Woking?'

'Yes. Why?'

'Just curiosity.' His father had died six months ago, he had said. And yet, since then, Mr Groenewald had written repeatedly to Abel Dixon in Woking about the children. Letters which must have been opened and read by the son of the same name, for Mr Groenewald had said that he had proof of their safe receipt. But those letters had been ignored – until the news broke that a diamond had been picked up in the veld near by.

'Are you married, Mr Dixon?' Shelagh asked.

'Alas, no. But if you are fearing that the children will suffer for lack of a woman's care—'

'Just what *are* your plans for the children?' she interrupted bluntly.

'In the first place, of course, I shall take them to England—'

Rina gave a small cry at this, and Hannes spoke truculently. 'We don't want to go to England with you!'

Just for an instant Abel Dixon's eyes seemed to lose their expression of selfless benevolence, and harden. Then he smiled at Hannes. 'Of course you do! You'll go to a boarding-school, you and your brother, where you'll learn to play rugby and cricket and have the time of your lives!'

'And what,' Shelagh asked with polite interest, 'are your plans for Rina?'

'I shall employ a governess for her, of course—'

'It will all cost you a great deal of money,' she observed.

'What is money, Miss Maybury, compared with the happiness and the welfare of three orphaned children?' he demanded piously.

Rina began to weep. 'I don't—want—to go anywhere—if Joy and Shelagh can't come too!' she sobbed.

Abel Dixon frowned at Shelagh. 'I recognise

your own charming and unusual name from the notary's letters, but who is Joy?'

'The children's half-sister, and mine.'

'The notary explained in one of his letters that Maria had married your father,' Dixon said thoughtfully. 'But he neglected to mention that there was a child of the marriage. Would—er—would Joy have inherited an interest in the farm?'

'No. Maria died in giving birth to her, so there was never any opportunity for her to include Joy in her will.'

A spasm of what was clearly relief crossed Dixon's face, and told Shelagh all she had needed to know about his motives. He gave her a gentle smile. 'Since the baby is your half-sister, Miss Maybury, you are obviously the person who will wish to have custody of her, and I wouldn't dream of trying to deprive you of her.'

Shelagh looked at him grimly. 'You brought up the matter of the farm. Are you, perhaps, planning to sell it?'

'Well, it wouldn't be of much practical use to the three children when they are living in England, would it?'

At this, Rina began to weep even more bitterly. She pushed aside her two brothers, who were trying to comfort her, and ran from the house.

Abel Dixon made a rueful gesture, indicating that the child would soon get over her distress. A gleam entered his wide blue eyes as he returned to the subject of the farm.

'I met a man in Hopetown who is forming a syndicate for the purpose of buying up land in the area, and I understand that this farm will fetch upwards of six thousand pounds. Of course,' he added hastily, 'the money would be invested for the children.'

'Of course,' Shelagh murmured. 'Tell me, Mr Dixon—have you discussed your plans with the notary in Hopetown?'

'No, for he was away on business when I reached the town, and so I came on here to make the acquaintance of my wards—'

He stopped. Luke towered in the doorway, looking large and grim and menacing. Rina was clinging to his arm, and her two brothers automatically moved so that they, too, were standing close to him as if for protection.

Deliberately, Luke addressed the children. 'You boys had better go and see to the cows. It looked to me as if they were trying to get into the vegetable-patch. And Rina, isn't that the baby I can hear whimpering?'

When the three children were out of earshot, Luke addressed Shelagh. 'Rina asked me to come. She seems to believe that she and her brothers are about to be taken to England by force.'

Abel Dixon was regarding him with distaste. Luke had obviously come straight from the trench which he was digging, for his skin was coated with red dust. The other man's fastidious gaze travelled over Luke's dishevelled hair, taking in the shirt unbuttoned almost to his waist so that his tanned, hard-muscled chest was exposed.

'Who,' he asked distantly, 'is this man, Miss Maybury?'

A demoralising weakness had filled her at sight of Luke. She wished she could remember that he was her enemy, that he had threatened her. More than anything she wished her treacherous heart could remember that Diana was installed on the other side of the barbed-wire fence, sharing his life.

'His name is Luke Valentine,' she answered Dixon, and added with deliberate malice, 'He is digging for diamonds on the farm.'

'What!' Abel Dixon's face flushed. He glared at Luke. 'Is that really what you're doing?'

'I'm damned if I know how it concerns you,' Luke said curtly, 'but yes, that *is* what I'm doing.'

'It concerns me, sir,' Dixon cried, stumbling to his feet, 'because I am the children's guardian, and if you have found any diamonds then I must demand that you hand them over to me! And I should like to know, too, who gave you the right to dig on the farm!'

'Mr Groenewald, the notary, leased him the mining rights,' Shelagh interrupted.

'Well, I intend to put a stop to it! If there are diamonds here, then they are the property of the children and of—'

'And of yourself?' Luke put in with contempt. He gave Dixon a long, appraising stare. 'I think you'll find that the mining rights are quite legally leased to me, and that they can't be withdrawn. I took the precaution of securing a six-month option.'

'I'm selling the farm to a syndicate!' Dixon cried triumphantly. 'The change of ownership will automatically invalidate your lease!'

'Oh yes?' Luke's tone was grim. 'Has Miss Maybury told you that she owns an integral piece of the farm, which she is refusing to sell?'

'No,' Shelagh answered for him, and smiled faintly at Luke. Almost miraculously, they were allies at that moment, and it was a very sweet experience. 'I thought I would allow him to enjoy his fool's paradise for a little longer,' she explained.

Dixon looked from one to the other, his expression wary now with mingled anxiety and disbelief. 'How *could* she own part of the farm? It was left by Maria to her three older children!'

Briefly, Shelagh told him the facts, and took pleasure in the dismay which shifted over Abel Dixon's almost girlishly beautiful face. When she had finished, he said defiantly, 'I don't see why it should make any difference to the syndicate. They aren't interested in a farmhouse and outbuildings. They simply want to dig for diamonds. They'll be prepared to pay six thousand pounds for the children's share of the farm—'

'No, they won't,' Shelagh interrupted. 'Why should they, when they could buy other, complete, farms in the area for the same money? Besides, my piece of land includes the well, which is the only source of water on the farm, and you may be very sure that I shall let any would-be purchaser of the children's share know that they would be denied access to my well!'

'So you see,' Luke added with satisfaction, 'you might as well relinquish your guardianship of the children and go back to England, for you won't get rich through them. I pay twenty guineas a month for the mining rights, and that is as much as you are likely to get your hands on!'

'We'll see!' Dixon shouted furiously. 'I'm going back to Hopetown now, to consult the notary and to negotiate with the syndicate! You haven't heard the last of the matter, either of you!'

He stormed from the house. Shelagh experienced no sense of triumph; instead, a weight of depression settled upon her.

'He may be right,' she said. 'The syndicate may be prepared to buy the children's share of the farm alone, and not care that there is no water-supply. And then he'll take the children to England, and in spite of his grandiose talk of boarding-schools and governesses, I'm quite certain that he'll send them to the first convenient workhouse while he enjoys their money . . .'

'Don't worry,' Luke reassured her. 'Dixon was wrong when he said that a change of ownership would invalidate my mining rights. A syndicate may well be prepared to buy part of the farm, but they wouldn't consider it while the right to dig on Mooifontein is not unencumbered.'

'Are you sure—' she began eagerly, turning to him, and as she did so her hand brushed against his where it rested upon the table. His fingers curled around her own.

'Quite sure,' he said, but his gaze locked with hers, and the language of their eyes was not concerned with mining rights or syndicates or even with the children.

Slowly, she moved, answering the unspoken, urgent summons of his eyes. He placed his hand on top of her head, tilting it back. Then he stooped, and his mouth travelled from her throat to her lips in a slow, lingering kiss, sending small currents of rapture along her nerve-ends and clouding her senses.

Something in the back of her mind nagged at her to push him away from her, but her limbs felt heavy and langourous, and all her willpower seemed to drain away as his kiss grew in passion.

He lifted his head, but did not let her go. 'Shelagh—' he began softly.

'Yes?' Her response was a whisper.

He hesitated. Deliberately, it seemed to her, he veiled his eyes with his lashes, so that she was no longer drowning in their message of longing and desire, and when he spoke again his words had the effect of a pailful of icy water flung full in her face.

'Let me excavate that shallow depression where your kitchen-garden is planted,' he said. 'Quickly, before Dixon has time to forge new schemes—'

Now, too late, she remembered what it was her subconscious had been trying to remind her of. Violently, she pushed at his chest.

'Oh God, how could I have forgotten?' she cried with rage and anguish. 'Leave me alone, Luke! Go back to your wife and leave me alone!'

He took hold of her shoulders, forcing her to look at him. 'I want to tell you the truth about Diana and me—'

'I know all about Diana and you, Luke! She is living with you in a tent beyond the barbed-wire fence, and if you think I am naive or stupid enough to believe that you are living in anything but marital intimacy—'

'I loathe and despise her, Shelagh,' he said quietly.

'And you've never touched her, not once?' Shelagh taunted angrily. 'All that beauty, so available, so desirable, and you've never been tempted—'

He shook her, his own eyes clouded with anger now. 'You're a child, Shelagh! You see everything in black and white, diffused by a romantic haze! What do you know of the breaking-point of a man, or of his many motivations? She goaded me once, yes—only once—into losing my self-control, but I took her in rage and contempt—'

'I don't want to hear!' Shelagh cried, clapping her hands to her ears. 'Get out of here, Luke, with your lies! You're worse—far worse—than Abel Dixon, because you're cleverer than he is, more plausible, and you're prepared to stop at nothing! You'd exploit anyone, any situation, to get the fortune you're after! You will even defame and besmirch your wife if you think it might persuade me to let you dig up my land for diamonds!'

He uttered a harsh, mirthless laugh. 'Let me tell you why Diana followed me here—'

'No! I don't want to hear any more of your lies! Whatever her reasons were, she is devoted enough to stay in this bleak country, to live with you in a tent without comfort or luxuries of any kind! I think I despise you most of all, Luke, for your contemptible, back-stabbing treachery towards your wife!'

He looked at her, his face gaunt and his eyes bleak. But he made no further attempt to justify himself, and left without a word.

In the days which followed there was no sign of Abel Dixon's return, so that the children began to lose their air of haunted anxiety. Luke set foot on Shelagh's piece of land only when he came to collect water from the well, and as she took care to be inside the house at the times when he called there was no further communication between them. Diana, looking beautiful and bored, continued to sit in the shade during the day, leafing through a journal or simply staring into space.

Life for Shelagh and the children went on as normally as it was possible to be, enclosed in a barbed-wire fence. In the shallow depression which Luke coveted so desperately, the vegetables they had planted were growing promisingly, and the livestock did not, after all, suffer too much for having to be driven daily through the narrow gap in the fence towards their grazing. Shelagh was glad, now, that the fence was there, for Hannes had fashioned a gate to fit the gap, and it all served to deter the dozens of prospectors who called at Mooifontein to ask permission to dig. When they saw the fence and the gate they made a detour to Luke's camp instead, and he invariably gave them short shrift.

One morning Shelagh saw that he had hitched his mules to the wagon, and shortly afterwards he drove away. Diana was not with him. Shelagh did not have to wonder for long where he had gone, or why he hadn't taken his wife with him, for that afternoon Diana arrived unexpectedly at the farmhouse.

The boys were out in the fields, hoeing the mealies, and Rina was weeding the vegetable patch. Shelagh had just finished feeding Joy and was changing her when Diana called.

'I know I'm not welcome,' Luke's wife said frankly as she sat down opposite Shelagh. 'But I shall go mad unless I speak to another human being. The two Griquas whom Luke hired to guard the farm know no English.'

Shelagh tried to hide the fact that she was stunned and unnerved by Diana's visit, and concentrated on ministering to the baby. 'Where has he gone?' she asked in as neutral a tone as she could manage.

'To Hopetown. He has found a few small stones, and wants to sell them in order to buy more supplies.'

'I see.' Shelagh darted a glance at her. 'Why—why did you not go with him?'

'He said we couldn't afford to stay in the hotel, and that he means to sleep on the wagon,' Diana said, discontent in her voice. After a small pause, she burst out, 'I am so *sick* of this benighted country! Sick of the heat and the dust and the flies! Sick of dusty, sweat-stained men with nothing on their minds but digging for diamonds!'

'You must have guessed before you came how it would be,' Shelagh observed.

'I didn't. I had no conception. I thought there would at least be towns, some kind of civilisation . . .'

Shelagh felt a twinge of pity for her. This beautiful creature, with her modish gowns and pampered complexion, was completely out of her element in the dour sun-scorched veld.

'What made you come, Mrs Valentine?' Shelagh asked impulsively, and then flushed. 'Of course, I understand that you must have wanted to be with your husband again—'

Diana uttered a grating laugh. When Shelagh looked swiftly at her, she sketched a half-mocking, half-defeated gesture. 'Oh, what does it matter? At first I pretended to the world that I'd come to be reconciled with Luke. But I'm bored with keeping up that façade. I came because I had no choice.'

'No choice?' Shelagh stared at her. Surely, women like Diana *always* had a choice?'

'I fell from grace,' Luke's wife explained in tones of bitter cynicism.

'I don't understand—'

'No, you wouldn't. You're a child, an innocent—for all that you've become involved with my husband. Oh, don't bother to deny it! I caught you together that night in the hotel, remember, and I haven't missed the tormented looks he casts in your direction whenever he catches sight of you from a distance!'

'Mrs Valentine—' Shelagh began, flushing.

'There's no need to look so guilty. I don't care. I'm his wife, and he's stuck with me, and the two of you will just have to go on eating your hearts out, because I'll never let him go!'

Stiffly, Shelagh said, 'You'll have to excuse me

now. I'm going to put the baby down for her nap, and then I have to feed the chickens.'

Diana left then, but all afternoon snatches of her disclosures echoed through Shelagh's mind, refusing to make sense.

'I pretended to the world that I'd come to be reconciled with Luke . . . I had no choice . . . fell from grace . . . I'll never let him go . . .'

Too late, Shelagh regretted that she had dismissed Diana while the latter was in a mood for confidences. Now she would probably never learn the truth about Luke's marriage.

But the next day, at the same time, Diana called at the house again, and this time she brought with her a gown which she was mending. And because she was bored and lonely, because she wanted to comfort herself by recalling past triumphs, and because Shelagh was the only audience available to her, she began to talk freely about her past.

'How well I recall the first time I wore this gown,' she sighed, looking up from the flounce she was mending. 'It was at a garden party at Buckingham Palace, and one of the royal dukes complimented me upon my looks. Indeed, I remember that was the first time he really noticed me. There are not many females, you know, who can boast of the love of a royal duke. But then, I was said to be the most beautiful débutante of my year.'

Shelagh sat very still. The royal duke who had wished to make Diana his mistress, and who had insisted that she should be married first, for the sake of discretion . . . It had all been true, then.

As if she were closely following Shelagh's

thoughts, Diana continued, 'There was hardly a young man I knew who did not wish to marry me. And although it was necessary for me to marry well, because I was the youngest of a large family and my parents were not wealthy, I don't think I would have married anyone when I did if it wasn't for a particular circumstance—'

'I think I understand,' Shelagh said quietly when Diana paused. 'The love of the royal duke made it necessary.'

'So Luke has told you about that,' Diana commented casually. 'I dare say you were suitably shocked. In Society it shocked no one. These arrangements are understood by the sophisticated. The mistake I made was in choosing Luke as my husband, simply because he was the one who appealed to me the most. When he found out about the duke, and that our marriage was to be a smokescreen, he behaved in the most provincial manner possible, and created a scandal by leaving me.'

Diana spread her hands. 'Even his family couldn't persuade him to see sense. They were ashamed of the embarrassment he was causing the royal family, and threatened to cut him off with a penny unless he went back to me. Instead, he left for India, to seek his own fortune.'

'And you and the duke—?'

'Oh, we had to be painfully discreet, of course, but it did not seriously affect our relationship.' Diana stared wistfully out of the window, at the drab veld. 'You would scarcely believe the luxury of my life. I had a house in Mayfair, and a place in the country. The duke paid all my bills. And then—I fell from grace.'

'What *did* you do?' Shelagh asked, overcome by curiosity at the phrase.

'I committed the unpardonable sin of having a love affair with someone outside my own class,' Diana said with caustic cynicism, 'and being found out.'

'But—' Shelagh began, confused. 'What had happened to the duke?'

'Bless your innocence, child! Nothing had happened to the duke. This was quite a separate little adventure of mine. Royalty can be very boring, you know, when the novelty has worn off. I needed some diversion, and I found it in the shape of my footman. He was quite the most gorgeous young man I had seen in a long while. Unfortunately he fell deeply and tediously in love with me, so I had to end the association and dismiss him. The fool killed himself, and left a suicide note explaining his reasons in lurid detail.'

Shelagh was too deeply shocked to say anything. She heard Diana go on with a sense of bitter injury, 'The contents of the note were made public and there was the most frightful scandal. The newspapers hounded me; my so-called friends dropped me, and the duke abandoned me and let it be known that he would no longer be responsible for my bills. I was not only ruined and friendless, but destitution was staring me in the face, for I had always lived above my means and had no savings.'

Shelagh looked at her, appalled. 'And so you decided to come and join Luke . . .'

'I had no choice. I had to leave England, and give people time to forget. Luke is my passport back to respectability and a place in Society. And that, my dear child, is why I intend to cling to him like grim death, no matter what I have to endure in the meantime. One day, when he has either found his fortune or has grown tired of seeking it, he will take me back to London; he will be accepted back into the good graces of his family and friends, and as his wife I shall be able to resume my role in Society, the scandal forgiven.'

Sickened, Shelagh once again found an excuse to get rid of Diana, and the next day she took care not to encourage another visit or further confidences by joining the boys in the fields and leaving Rina to give the baby her afternoon feed.

She could scarcely bear to contemplate the story which Diana had told her so casually, with such a lack of repentance or shame. She shivered whenever she recalled how Diana had said, 'I mean to cling to Luke like grim death.' What an unspeakable situation for him to be trapped in!

With deep remorse, Shelagh recalled the insults she herself had flung at him, and how she had accused him of defaming and besmirching his wife. As if it were possible to defame or besmirch someone like Diana!

At the end of the week Shelagh saw Luke's wagon swaying along the track in the veld, and she could only guess at his feelings as he returned to his wife and his mockery of a marriage.

He spent no time with Diana, however, but strode straight to the farmhouse when he alighted from the wagon. Shelagh, her heart full of the many things she wished to say to him, hurried outside to meet him.

There was no pleasure in his face as he regarded her. His eyes communicated no language of desire or love, but were flat and impersonal.

'I have some news for you,' he said grimly.

Her heart began to beat fast with foreboding. 'What—what is it?'

'You will remember that I told you the syndicate would refuse to buy the children's share of the farm once they realised that I have a six-month option on the mining rights?'

'Yes—'

'Well, their appetite was whetted by the news that I had found some insignificant stones on Mooifontein, and they made Abel Dixon an offer. They also suggested to him the one way in which he would be able to get me to release those mining rights.'

'What—what was that?' Shelagh asked fearfully, when Luke paused for breath. 'What happened?'

'He increased the rental of the rights to a thousand guineas a month.'

Shelagh's mouth was dry with shock. Luke could not possibly pay such a sum; *no one* would dream of paying such an outrageous sum even if they could afford it. So now Luke would have to withdraw, and Dixon would sell the children's share of the farm to the syndicate. And the three children would have to leave for an unknown fate in a country foreign to them, with a guardian who was interested only in their money and who would almost certainly abandon them once they had served their purpose.

'Well,' she said flatly, 'that is that, then.'

'Not quite.' He gave her a smile of weary triumph. 'I did the only thing *I* could do to thwart them all. I sub-leased mining rights on Mooifontein to two hundred other prospectors at five guineas a month each in order to raise the rental.'

'Oh! But—but that's wonderful—'

'Not quite so wonderful,' Luke said soberly, 'when you realise that, by the end of next week, you and the children and the livestock will be marooned on your piece of Mooifontein, surrounded by two hundred prospectors and their families digging trenches on every spare inch of land around you.'

CHAPTER EIGHT

A HUNDRED questions were buzzing through Shelagh's mind, but before she could voice any of them she saw that Diana had emerged from their tent, and was watching her and Luke with a cynical smile.

'*The two of you will just have to go on eating your hearts out*,' Diana's taunt echoed maliciously in her brain, '*because I'll never let him go . . .*'

Even though their meeting was quite innocent, their conversation impersonal, Shelagh felt as degraded by that knowing little smile as if Luke's wife had caught them in a compromising situation.

She said hastily, 'Well—so long as the prospectors don't trespass on my piece of land . . .' and turned to go back to the house.

'Shelagh—' Luke's voice detained her. 'The important thing is that the three children are safe. Dixon won't sell the farm and whisk them off to some workhouse in England.'

She nodded, and then said fearfully, 'But what if he should retaliate by increasing the rental even more, to such an impossible sum that even two hundred sub-lessees couldn't help you raise the money?'

'He won't risk killing the goose that lays the golden eggs,' Luke said with a grim smile. 'After all, he'll be receiving a steady income of a thousand guineas a month. In six months he will have earned more than the purchase price the syndicate were prepared to pay for the farm.'

It was galling to know that the despicable Dixon would be profiting in this way through the children, but as Shelagh returned to the house she comforted herself with the thought that the three of them were indeed safe, and would not be forced into exile by their guardian. Everything else seemed unimportant by comparison. She could even put up with the two hundred families who would be coming to over-run them at the end of the following week.

But Luke had been wrong about two things. The prospectors to whom he had sub-leased mining rights on Mooifontein did not bring with them the civilising influence of their families, and neither did they wait until they could legally take up their claims before they arrived at the farm.

That same afternoon a dense cloud of dust on the horizon heralded the vanguard, and they continued to arrive the next day like locusts descending upon a field of corn.

They travelled by every conceivable means of conveyance, each hopeful fortune-seeker dressed according to his former station in life. There were erstwhile sailors who had jumped ship in Cape Town to follow the lure of diamonds, and who still wore their yellow oilskins and rubber boots; former cheapjack salesmen with garish clothes and loud, boastful voices; young men of good family who were already becoming coarsened by their greed and by their surroundings; experienced miners in canvas suits and stiff leather boots; evangelists who had come to combine preaching with diamond-grubbing; former clerks and farmers; gamblers, rogues and speculators.

Forming a hotch-potch community, they took up position along the perimeter of Mooifontein, beyond the double barbed-wire fence with which Luke had had the farm enclosed. Shelagh and the children could see them, hovering there like vultures waiting for a kill, each time they went to work in the mealie-fields, or when they went to drive the stock back from grazing. It was a disquieting, even a sinister, sight.

Each prospector hoped to be first on Mooifontein when the time came to take up their rights, and so grab the pick of the claims. Their feverish eagerness, their diamond-hunger, was an almost tangible thing, and Shelagh shivered as she contemplated what would happen when Luke finally opened a gap in the outer barbed-wire fence to let them in.

It was Hannes who spelled out to her the practical disasters which were likely to accompany the forthcoming rush.

He had come in from working in the mealie-fields, watching by that restless, impatient mob. 'Shelagh,' he said with a frown, 'how are we going to stop them from trampling all over the mealie-fields? They won't care about anything except to get to the bit of ground where they think there are likely to be diamonds. If there happens to be a short cut through the mealies, they'll take it.'

'Yes . . .' She chewed at her lip. 'I'll have to go and speak to Luke. He must work out some orderly system for letting them in.'

Forcing herself to brave Diana's amused, cynical gaze, she went to the tent after she had failed to find Luke working in his trench. But he was not at the camp either, and Diana did not know when to expect him back. He and his two Griqua labourers, it appeared, were constantly patrolling Mooifontein's perimeter, inspecting the barbed-wire fence and ensuring that none of the prospectors sneaked through before he was legally entitled to do so, and thereby provoke bloodshed from the enraged competitors.

'Although, if you ask me,' Diana added moodily, '*anything* which would enliven matters in this boring place is to be welcomed!'

When Shelagh finally glimpsed Luke riding back to his camp several afternoons later, he looked tired and grim, and it was clear that he had abandoned the check on the fences only because the sky looked black and threatening and the coming thunderstorm would deter the rapacious waiting mass from anything other than seeking shelter.

Shelagh stood at the gate which Hannes had fashioned for the fence which surrounded her own *morgen* of land, and called to Luke.

'I wish to speak to you,' she said formally, when he approached.

His eyes still wore that flat, impersonal look with which he had regarded her ever since she had told him that she despised him; a look which formed an insuperable barrier between them.

'What is it?' he asked, equally formally.

Shelagh began to explain the need for letting the prospectors on to Mooifontein in an orderly fashion, because of the risk to the young mealie-plants in the fields. Her voice was suddenly drowned by an explosion of thunder; the earth felt as if a giant hand had seized it and shaken it, and jagged lightning snaked across a cobalt sky. At the same moment huge raindrops began to strike the ground, filling the air with the pungent smell of wet earth.

Luke's gaze measured the distance to the farm-house. Then, above another fearsome clap of thunder, he shouted, 'Make for the barn! Quickly!'

She stumbled as she ran, blinded by what was now a cloudburst, and his arm enclosed her waist, half-carrying, half-dragging her towards the barn. Inside they collapsed, breathless, against a stack of hay left over from the animals' winter feed supplies.

Shelagh's hair, soaked by the torrential down-pour, had come down and she made ineffectual attempts to wring the water from it. She glanced up, and saw that Luke was pulling his shirt over his head. The wet skin of his shoulders and chest, tanned by constant exposure to the sun, gleamed like polished bronze. She fought an almost over-whelming yearning to reach out and move her palms over his wet flesh.

He took a step towards her, and matter-of-factly began to towel her hair with his shirt, his move-ments brisk and as impersonal as such a very per-sonal service could possibly be. But her simple gown, made over from one of Maria's dresses, clung wetly to her body, moulding itself to her breasts and thighs, and she could witness his self-restraint crumbling as his gaze travelled over her. He was still engaged in drying her hair, but his movements had now become slow and lingering. With her head held between his hands she looked up at him, and was seized by a wave of emotion which was almost like physical pain.

'Luke?' she whispered.

He grew still. His eyes were veiled by his lashes, his gaze fixed upon her mouth. 'Yes, Shelagh,' he responded with taut self-control. 'What is it you want?'

'I want—*you*—' The confession was almost inaudible.

'Do you think—I don't feel the same way?' His voice was hoarse.

'Then take me.'

'*No!* I'm a married man, in case you've forgotten—'

'I know about Diana, Luke. She doesn't merit any loyalty from you. And she'll never let you go. So let us have what little we are able—'

A muffled sound escaped him, and he shook his head blindly. Then, with a sudden, violent gesture, he threw the wet shirt on the ground and pulled her hungrily against him, and together they sank down on to the stack of hay.

They were oblivious of the elements raging outside as their lips fused in mutual need and passion, their bodies entwined in an intimacy which was as passionately heady as it was potentially dangerous.

She lowered her head, and covered his naked chest with light feathery kisses which forced a groaning sound from him. He took hold of her wet hair, calling a halt to the emotions which were threatening to sweep them away.

'No, Shelagh! We've gone far enough.' His voice was muffled and almost unrecognisable. 'I won't make you my mistress—not with the children sharing your life, and with Diana on your doorstep, capable of doing you whatever harm her evil mind could think of. So—*no more!*'

He heaved himself away from her and picked up his discarded shirt, wringing it out and pulling it over his head again. He sat down, putting as great a physical distance as possible between them while still enabling them to make themselves heard above the sound of the storm.

'You said that you knew about Diana, Shelagh. What do you know, and how?'

'I know everything. She told me herself.' As his eyes narrowed in disbelief, Shelagh explained, 'She was bored and lonely, and so she visited the house, and told me why she came to join you.'

He uttered a growl of remembered rage and defeat. 'Oh, she was so damnably clever . . . She knew that I had grounds for divorcing her after the public scandal of her affair with the footman. And so she set about destroying those grounds quickly, before I could find out about the scandal.'

'I don't understand,' Shelagh said, puzzled.

'No, few people would. But Diana made a point of consulting a lawyer before she left England, and arming herself with information regarding the divorce laws. It seems that if it could be proved that I had forgiven her the affair, that I had taken her back and that we had become totally reconciled, I could not at a later date use her adultery as grounds for petitioning for divorce.'

Bitterness entered his voice. 'And so she cut the ground from under my feet by asking for a hotel room in our joint names, and by telling all and sundry that we had been reconciled and were making a fresh start. And because I did not know what her motive was, because I disliked the thought of washing dirty linen in public, I did nothing to contradict her. Now the damage has been done. If I tried to divorce her at this stage, she could produce overwhelming circumstantial evidence to support her claim that I had forgiven her and taken her back as my wife.'

'But,' Shelagh objected, 'if you were to explain that you knew nothing of the scandal—?'

He uttered a crack of corrosive laughter. 'I'd find that very hard to prove. The scandal had been reported in the British newspapers, and Hopetown was full of Englishmen who had left home at the same time as Diana and who recognised her. But no one was bold or brave enough to bring the subject up in my hearing, and I thought it was simply her extraordinary beauty which was causing all the stares and the whispers. No, I could never hope to prove that I remained in ignorance while so many others around us in Hopetown knew all about Diana.'

Shelagh was silent for a while. Then, quietly, she formed a question which had been burning into her brain for a long time. 'Luke, why did you bring Diana to Mooifontein, to share your tent? Was it just to put pressure on me?'

'It was a matter of stark economic necessity,' he said. 'I simply could not afford to let her stay at the hotel. She had left enormous debts behind her—debts for which I, as her husband, was still legally responsible. Once I had sent off drafts to her major creditors I had next to nothing left.'

His voice took on a note of intensity. 'I need money, Shelagh. A great deal of money. It's the only means by which I shall ever be free of her. If I could afford to instal her in some society where her past is not known; in New York, perhaps . . . I could then persuade her to divorce me for desertion in return for a generous allowance.'

Shelagh said nothing. If Luke made his fortune, she knew Diana would not settle for New York, or for life anywhere as a divorced woman, no matter how wealthy. She would settle for nothing less than a triumphal return to London Society as the reformed and chastened wife of Luke Valentine, for whose sake she would have to be forgiven past sins.

But Luke did not appear to realise this, and it seemed too cruel to rob him of his only glimmer of hope. Shelagh decided to change the subject.

'The storm is passing over, and the children will be anxious about me, imagining that I had been caught in it. There's something I have to discuss with you, Luke. You will have to let the prospectors in one by one when the time comes, for otherwise they will trample the young mealies out of existence—'

He cut her short, astonishment in his voice. 'Didn't you understand, Shelagh? There'll be no mealie-fields left in existence once I have to let the prospectors in. All of Mooifontein's land—the mealie-fields, the grazing pastures—*everything* will be included in the two hundred claims the prospectors have come to take up.'

'No, I didn't understand,' she said with dismay. 'I remember, you once told me specifically that the lease prohibited interference with cultivated land or with grazing—'

'That was the original lease drawn up by Mr Groenewald, when he was acting on the children's behalf, and when I was the only one digging on Mooifontein. Be sensible, Shelagh. How did you imagine the farm could accommodate an extra two hundred prospectors if the cultivated fields and the pasturage were to be excluded?'

'But the lease stipulates—' she persisted stubbornly.

'It no longer does so. Dixon has the authority to waive the excluding clauses, and that is what he did.'

'Are you saying that he co-operated?' Shelagh demanded incredulously. 'Why should he have done that, when you were turning the tables on him and on the syndicate by sub-letting claims?'

Luke gave a sour laugh. 'He was very well pleased with the outcome of events, once he realised how much better off he would be than if he had sold the land to the syndicate outright. Of course he was glad to co-operate, and to remove any possible obstacles in the way of that income of a thousand guineas a month!'

Shelagh had the helpless feeling of having been crushed between two inexorable forces. She thought of the promising young mealies in the fields, over which she and the children had slaved so hard. And then she thought of their stock which were about to be deprived of grazing.

As if he were following her thoughts, Luke said, 'The stock will have to be slaughtered, Shelagh. I'll see to it as soon as I have the time.'

'No.' She freed herself from the embracing circle of his arm, and jumped to her feet. He rose, too, and took her by the shoulders.

'It's necessary, Shelagh. There is not enough grazing on your patch of land to support them for long.'

She said quietly, 'You realise, of course, that without mealie-fields and without stock the children and I face starvation . . .'

'Not if you'll let me dig up your vegetable-patch! I'm convinced there are enough diamonds there to make both of us rich beyond our wildest dreams?'

'The only certain source of food we'll have left,' she said in a dull voice, 'and you want to dig it up . . .'

He shook her angrily. 'You and the children won't starve! The thousand guineas a month Dixon will be getting belong to the three older children; he will be legally and morally bound to use some of it for their welfare. And in the meantime I could be excavating the depression where your vegetables are planted—'

'No,' she said quietly, with finality. 'I'm sorry, Luke.'

She walked away, leaving him cursing in a frustrated monotone, and went slowly towards the house. The sun shone once more from a clear blue sky and the once-thirsty land lay refreshed and revived beneath it. In a matter of days new grass would spring up for grazing, and the mealies would grow almost visibly in their fields . . .

She sighed. When Luke thought up his scheme to outwit Abel Dixon and the syndicate, she felt certain that he had had other motives besides preventing the children's guardian from taking them away with him to England. Luke had also foreseen that, with no mealie-fields and no stock, and with the prospect of starvation staring them in the face, Shelagh would agree at last to having the vegetable-patch excavated.

Once, she would have been enraged at the knowledge. But now she understood, and could readily forgive. Luke was driven by the need to find a fortune in diamonds. In the beginning it had merely been an overwhelming ambition with him, to show his family in England who had so cruelly and unfairly disowned and disinherited him that he could make his fortune in his own way. But now it was much more than that. It had become an almost fanatical, uncompromising force driving him on, because he believed it was the one way in which he could gain his freedom from Diana.

When Shelagh reached the farmhouse the children crowded anxiously in the kitchen doorway to welcome her.

'We feared you might have been struck by lightning,' Rina said.

Shelagh forced a smile. 'I took shelter in the barn.' She hesitated. 'Hannes, shall you and I go and see if the storm did any damage to the vegetables?'

He fell into step beside her, and she was grateful that he didn't chatter but allowed her to follow her own thoughts. Why, she asked herself for the hundredth time, was shc so stubbornly opposed to the thought of having the kitchen-garden dug up? If there really were a fortune in diamonds there, as Luke confidently believed, then she was being utterly stupid and irrational.

She could only put it down to instinct. A strong, almost primitive intuition that the vegetable-garden was important, and that keeping the stock alive for as long as she possibly could was equally important.

Some of the young plants had been washed out of the soil by the ferocity of the rain, and the ground needed firming round the cabbage seedlings. As Shelagh and Hannes worked together to restore matters, she said quietly, 'Tomorrow morning we must start pulling up the young mealies, and store the plants in the barn. They will have to be used for animal feed.'

He sat back on his haunches, staring at her in disbelief. With compassion, remembering the hard work he had put in on the mealie-fields, Shelagh explained the situation to him.

His face was pale and set when she finished, but all he said was, 'I don't know for how long we'll be able to keep the stock alive on this little patch of ground.'

'The rain was a godsend,' Shelagh said. 'During the days that are left for them to graze freely, they'll be able to build up condition on the new young grass. After that—we'll just have to do the best we can.'

In the interval before the prospectors were let on to Mooifontein, Shelagh and the children were frantically occupied in preparing for the coming state of siege. The mealie-plants were pulled up and stored in the barn, together with any other vegetation which could possibly be used for animal feed in an emergency. In the little spare time that was left, Hannes fashioned a heavy padlock for the gate so that they would not be encroached upon by the prospectors.

On the appointed day, the rush which followed when Luke and his Griqua labourers cut down the barbed-wire fence encircling Mooifontein was frightening to watch. Once again, Shelagh had cause to be grateful that he had also had her own small patch of land enclosed.

The prospectors swarmed like ants over the farm, frothing with greed and frantic enthusiasm, coming to blows as they fought for some favoured spot, pegging their claims with cairns of stone, hastening to erect signs printed in crude capitals showing their ownership and the licence number which entitled them to dig in that chosen spot.

On their *morgen* of land, Shelagh felt as though she and the children were shipwrecked in a sea of tents, wagons, oxen, camp-fires, and sweating, feverish humanity. All round them the veld lay choked by the dust of the excavations, and the sound of pick and shovel striking the earth became a daily monotonous rhythm.

Inevitably, because the only water-supply was on Shelagh's land, she was forced to give permission for the prospectors to draw from the well. They were made to line up in an orderly manner beyond the gate and let in one by one. In this way she was kept up to date with the progress of the diggers.

A few small diamonds had been found near the surface, but nothing to fire the imagination. Some of the men were becoming discouraged and were talking of pulling out, infecting others with their gloom. Every single article they required had to be paid for at an enormously inflated price from the salesmen who swarmed to the camp, and daily more and more diggers began to talk of cutting their losses and leaving.

Horrified as Shelagh had been at the rapacious rush on Mooifontein, her blood chilled at the thought of the prospectors pulling out. For if that happened, Abel Dixon would simply sell the land to the syndicate and take the three Steenkamp children with him to England to justify his pocketing the proceeds. And even if the syndicate no longer wished to buy land which had failed to yield any significant stones, she and the children would be no better off, for they would be surrounded by acres of useless crater-scarred land.

But then Luke, whose excavations had gone deeper than those of any of the newcomers, made an important discovery. Lying some fifty feet below the surface was a layer of yellow clay, and embedded in this he found several large diamonds. They were not of first-class quality, being of a yellowish tinge and containing imperfections, but they were a certain sign that the diamonds previously found near the surface had not merely been deposited there haphazardly by the movement of the earth over centuries.

Digging continued feverishly, and as more prospectors struck the yellow ground more diamonds were found, some of them of the finest water.

The news brought a further seething mass of prospectors to the area. Mr van Wyk, who owned the farm bordering on Mooifontein, fulfilled Mr Botha's prediction that some of the Boers would bow to Mammon, for he also began to lease claims on his farm, du Toit's Pan, so that the city of tents now extended beyond Mooifontein's boundary. With helpless consternation, Shelagh watched the disordered confusion mushrooming around her.

Daily, fortunes were made. Men who found substantial diamonds would spend the proceeds with unbelievable profligacy on almost anything which caught their fancy. Huge sums were staked on the turn of a card, on the rival speeds of two beetles in the dust, on almost any chance on which it was possible to wager. And if the fortune was lost, there was always the feeling that another huge diamond was waiting to be found.

Hot on the heels of the discovery of so many new diamonds came Abel Dixon. He arrived at the farmhouse, wrinkling his nose in disgust at the noise and the filth and the putrescence of the mining camp, and informed Shelagh that he had come to stay for a while.

'Why?' she asked bluntly.

'To become acquainted with my three tender charges, of course,' he answered piously, as if he had never shown his hand and all but admitted that his only interest in the children lay in whatever riches he might milk from them.

Shelagh was to discover that hypocrisy was Dixon's second nature, and that he practised it by habit even when it could gain him nothing. She also learnt, before long, that it was greed which had brought him to Mooifontein. The news of all those diamonds being discovered had stirred his envy, and he was no longer content with his thousand guineas a month. He wished to discover if there were other possible ways of increasing his fortunes.

With frightening speed the landscape around Shelagh and the children altered. Now that it was known that significant stones existed in the clay, some of the diggers sent for their families and began to put up dwellings in place of their tents.

Luke was among those who spent his first profits in this way. Shelagh, watching his dwelling take shape, knew that his sole motive was the desire to put a greater physical distance between himself and Diana, and her heart contracted when she thought of his empty, hollow, marriage and how it would stand for ever in their path.

Because there were no bricks to be had, the dwellings were little more than shacks of wooden frames, with corrugated iron roofs and mere holes for windows. The dwellings themselves accentuated the ugliness and the sordid feculence of the camp.

Diamond-dealers arrived and set up offices in one-roomed tin hovels. Brothels sprang up and so did doss-houses. The roads were no more than linked open spaces winding between the shacks and hovels and tents, drained on each side by wide, dirty ditches. Across these dykes, filled with stinking, stagnant drain-water and sewage, planks gave access to the doors of the buildings.

And those who lived in this unbelievable squalor would, when they found valuable diamonds, spend their money in mindless, reckless frenzy on anything which offered, so that the itinerant salesmen grew rich.

Diana's reaction to the mining city was a curious one. She began to behave like some great medieval lady moving among her serfs. Immaculately dressed, with an air of dignity bordering on hauteur, she would move through the settlement of canvas and corrugated iron, pretending to be blind to the corruption and squalor around her. She kept herself aloof from the other women in the camp, but if she heard that one of them was ailing she would set out to visit her. At first Diana's exquisite beauty had drawn bold stares and lascivious remarks from the men, but her glance of freezing disdain had soon quelled even those who knew of her past, and now they invariably bowed respectfully whenever she crossed their path.

Abel Dixon had taken a dislike to Diana. 'Madam High-and-Mighty', he snorted as he watched her set out at a regal pace from her dwelling, obviously on some charitable mission. 'Who does she think she is?'

Diana had, of course, snubbed him when he tried to impress her with his spurious charm. But Shelagh had other things besides Diana Valentine on her mind. They were coming to the last of the mealie-meal; there was very little sugar or flour left, and it would be some weeks before they could start harvesting the vegetables from the kitchen-garden. Worse, the cows were beginning to exhibit the effects of their restricted diet and were yielding very little milk. The prospect of having to let the children go hungry was very real and imminent.

Abruptly, Shelagh addressed Abel Dixon. 'You have now received at least one month's rent of a thousand guineas. Some of that money should be spent for the children's benefit, because it really belongs to them.'

He gave her a limpid look. 'Of course it belongs to them! But it has all been snugly invested for their future benefit.'

She bit her lip. 'There are things which they need *now*. If Mr Groenewald were to hear that they are suffering hardship, I am sure there are ways in which the law could compel you to spend money on their welfare—'

'My dear Miss Maybury,' he interrupted gently, 'if *I* thought the children were suffering hardship under your care, I know where my duty would lie. I should have to send them away, to some place where I know they would be better cared for.'

The threat was unmistakable. If Shelagh tried to

bring pressure to bear on him, he would despatch the children to some institution in England, and then forget about them.

He went on in a silky voice, 'I should naturally be sorry to have to do that, for I know how fond you are of them.'

Burning with impotent rage, she walked out of the house. As usual, there was a steady stream of diggers lining up to draw water at the well. Shelagh toyed for a while with the notion of charging them for the water, and then abandoned it reluctantly. Even though the newly-rich ones were more than able to pay, and their money would be better spent on water than on exorbitantly expensive gimcrack goods from the itinerant salesmen, it seemed morally wrong to her to demand payment for a natural resource which she was fortunate enough to possess.

The miners acknowledged her with polite deference. She was something of an enigma to them, living in the farmhouse with the children, remaining detached and aloof from the activities of the camp. While many of the younger men regarded her with admiration, none of them felt bold enough to attempt familiarity.

Her heart quickened when she saw that Luke, too, was waiting to draw water, and she moved towards him. He had been so busy, working his claim and constructing his dwelling, that she had scarcely seen or spoken to him since that afternoon in the barn.

'Have you found any more diamonds?' she asked him.

He grinned tiredly. 'Only of sufficient value to continue living from hand to mouth. And speaking of living from hand to mouth—I see that you have succeeded so far in keeping all your stock alive.'

'Yes.' She hesitated. 'But I shan't be able to continue doing so for long. They're losing condition. We'll have to start slaughtering them soon, both to save them from starvation and also to save ourselves from a similar fate.'

'It's that bad?' He stared at her, and then burst out—'Shelagh, for the love of God, let me dig up your wretched kitchen-garden!'

'No. I always had an instinct about it, Luke, and I know now that I was right. Abel Dixon has no intention of spending on the children a farthing of the rental he receives. If I allowed you to dig up the vegetables and you found nothing, we really *would* face starvation. And if that happened, then public opinion—not to mention Mr Groenewald—would force Dixon to take some action on the children's behalf. What he would do, I have no doubt at all, is to despatch them to a workhouse in England, while pretending that he has sent them to his own home to be looked after by nannies and governesses.'

Luke swore impotently under his breath. 'And for how long do you suppose the vegetables would save you from starvation, Shelagh? A month or two—that's all! Even if you slaughtered your stock, and you and the older children subsisted on dried meat, what about the baby? *She* couldn't live on dried meat! You need money—hard cash—and the only way you'll get that is by allowing me to excavate the one spot where my instinct tells me there are diamonds to be found!'

'And *my* instinct tells me that I must hold on to my vegetable-patch at all costs, Luke.'

He shook his head with baffled anger. 'Well, at least charge Abel Dixon for his keep! That would help a little.'

Shelagh sighed. 'He would open his blue eyes very wide, and explain that every penny he has received is tied up for the children's benefit, and hint that if he isn't welcome perhaps he ought to leave and take the children with him . . .'

'Refuse to feed him,' Luke said brutally. 'He won't want to leave while the money is rolling in. As long as you still have food, charge him for it!'

'I couldn't,' Shelagh began, and broke off. A slow smile spread across her face as a solution to all her problems suddenly came to her. 'Yes, I *could*! Of course I could!'

'I don't know,' Luke said morosely, 'why you should suddenly look as if you had just stumbled upon the pot of gold at the foot of the rainbow—'

'But in a modest way, I have!' Shelagh was triumphant. 'And you have helped me to find it! I know what I have to do, now, for myself and the children to survive!'

He regarded her with a wary expression. 'And what is that?'

'I always told you, didn't I, Luke, that my kitchen-garden was important! With the vegetables, and by a judicious slaughtering of the stock, I intend to make a small fortune of my own!'

'You're planning to sell the produce? That could be—'

'I intend to do better than that!' she interrupted jubilantly. 'I'm going to turn the farmhouse into a superior eating-house for all those miners who have money to burn!'

CHAPTER NINE

Only two days later a hand-printed sign on the gate announced that, for the price of a half-sovereign, superior home-cooked dinners would be served to the public at the farmhouse that evening. All the miners who came to draw water at the well stopped to pore over the advertisement, and at sunset Shelagh was busy in the kitchen, nervously praying that at least some of the half-dozen places set at the table in the parlour would be filled.

Luke had helped Hannes to slaughter one of the bullocks, and while the bulk of the meat was being salted and hung for future use, a large rump roast was sizzling in the oven of the kitchen range. Shelagh planned to serve with it roast potatoes and glazed pumpkin, for the green vegetables in the garden were not yet ready for harvesting. A simple pudding of sweet dumplings in a cinnamon sauce would round off the meal.

Abel Dixon strolled into the kitchen, looking as foppishly elegant as usual, and sniffed the air appreciatively. 'When do the rest of us eat?' he wanted to know. 'From the smell of that beef, Miss Maybury, I vote we should dine before the customers arrive and demolish it all!'

Shelagh said calmly, 'The children and I will eat whatever is left, *if* anything is left. If you wish to be sure of dining on roast beef, Mr Dixon, then I'd advise you to reserve a place at the table and pay in advance for the meal. Hannes is taking the customers' money at the front door.'

Dixon's mouth tightened with chagrin, but he made no direct protest. Instead, he said with barely-concealed menace, 'I'm not sure that I approve of the involvement of my wards in this commercial enterprise. If the house is to be regularly invaded by rough uncouth miners, it may be desirable to have the children sent away . . .'

Shelagh was too tense and keyed-up to react to the veiled threat. What if no one should come, after all? What if the miners had decided that a half-sovereign was too exorbitant a sum to pay for a meal?

But they pay that for one single cabbage bought from the *smous*, she told herself.

Yes, a voice inside her head retorted, *but people have illogical attitudes. They may regard a cabbage as a necessity and roast beef and two vegetables as a luxury . . .*

'Shelagh!' Hannes's voice reached her from the front door, cutting into her thoughts. His cry had held a note of panic, and she left the stove to hurry to his side.

Dirkie, who had been stationed by the gate to let in would-be customers, was almost being crushed by the mob of miners who had arrived in answer to Shelagh's advertisement.

The evening threatened to become one of total

chaos, and at one point almost deteriorated into violence among the hungry miners. Shelagh summoned all her diplomacy and tact, and promised anyone who wished to wait until the first half-dozen customers had eaten that a meal would be made available to him, however late the hour.

While the children waited at the table, Shelagh stoked the range and roasted more beef, peeled more potatoes and brought another pumpkin out of store.

It was past midnight when the last diner left, and Shelagh and the children sat wearily down in the kitchen for a scratch meal of their own.

Hannes, who had been counting the takings, said, 'We've made twelve sovereigns, Shelagh.'

They were all far too tired to react with triumph. 'We can't repeat this every night,' Shelagh said. 'For one thing, we shall soon run out of fuel if I am to stoke the range for hours on end. What we ought to do is to cook large quantities at a time. But then,' she added despairingly, 'we shall still need to stoke the range in order to keep the food hot, for we simply cannot cope with more than six diners at a time!'

'We need more tables,' Hannes said.

'We need more of everything. Tables, chairs, crockery, cutlery . . . The list is endless. And we can't afford to buy from one of the *smous*, for they charge through the nose for everything.'

'There are some wooden boards stored in the barn,' Hannes said thoughtfully. 'I think I could make trestle tables.'

'Tables are useless without chairs,' Shelagh told

him with a note of defeat. 'And even your clever fingers wouldn't be able to fashion something as complicated as a chair.'

'No, but I *could* use some of the boards to make benches to fit the trestle tables.'

'And I'll make cushions for the benches!' Rina offered eagerly.

'I'll help!' Dirkie cried with enthusiasm. 'We could stuff them with dried mealie-leaves and old rags!'

Shelagh smiled tiredly at them. 'Yes, but where would we put the tables and benches? Even if we moved most of the furniture out of the parlour, there still wouldn't be room to take more than another half-dozen people.'

'Couldn't we use the *stoep*?' Dirkie offered.

The parlour door opened onto the *stoep*, the veranda area which ran along three sides of the house. It *would* be feasible to use it as if it were an extension of the parlour . . .

'Yes,' Shelagh conceded. 'That would answer. But it still leaves the problem of eating-utensils, and I really don't see how we are possibly to solve that . . .'

Silence followed her words, and she became aware that the two boys were staring significantly at their sister. Rina coloured, and jumped to her feet. 'I was going to tell her!' she cried angrily. 'If you two had stopped talking for a moment, and given me a chance—'

'Tell me what?' Shelagh asked, mystified.

'Come, I'll show you,' Rina said, glaring at her brothers and going to the door.

In the girl's bedroom, Shelagh helped Rina to manoeuvre a large wooden chest from beneath the bed.

'Ma said it was to be my dowry,' Rina explained as she opened the lid. 'She said she had never had a use for it, but that maybe one day *I* would. It all belonged to her mother, who brought it with her from Cape Town.'

As she spoke, she began to remove protective layers of faded paper from inside the chest, and Shelagh held the candle closer. Rina's dowry proved to include, among other household relics, an almost complete dinner-service of blue and white willow-patterned porcelain, manufactured during a period when it was customary to entertain on a lavish scale so that there was twenty-four of everything. And right at the bottom of the chest, darkened with age and neglect, were two canteens of silver cutlery.

Shelagh began to laugh helplessly as she thought of the rough, unpolished miners in their hobnailed boots and their neck-clothes dining off elegant porcelain, clutching silver forks in their work-hardened, calloused hands.

'Won't it do?' Rina asked anxiously.

'My dear child . . . It's much too good for the likes of the miners. *If* we could get it transported to somewhere like Cape Town, where people would be willing to pay what such beautiful old things are really worth, your dowry would fetch a good price, and therefore I can't risk having any of it damaged—'

'You said we had to have money if we were to

stay together,' Rina reminded her fiercely. 'I'd far sooner risk every piece of the dinner-service being smashed than have to go to England with that horrible Mr Dixon, and never see you or Joy again, Shelagh!'

She began to weep, partly with fatigue, and Shelagh kissed her tenderly. 'Very well. We'll use it for the eating-house. But our first profits will be spent in replacing it with more functional utensils so that your beautiful heirlooms may be safely packed away again.'

The next day Shelagh pinned a notice to the gate, announcing that she was suspending the service of meals for two evenings while work was being carried out on extending the eating-house. She and the children laboured, almost without pause, on putting their plans into practice. When they were finally ready to re-open, even the uncouth miners were temporarily overawed by the elegance which met their gaze.

Shelagh had found an old bedspread of heavy dark-blue material stored away in one of Maria's trunks, and this she had cut up for cloths to conceal the roughness of the trestle tables which Hannes had quickly nailed together. Against this dark background the lighter-blue and white of the dinner-service formed an enchanting contrast, and the old silver tableware had been polished with wood-ash until it gleamed in the light of the many candles which cast a soft, romantic glow over the *stoep*.

From the evidence of that night, the eating-house would be a resounding success. Shelagh stayed in the kitchen, cooking and dishing up the meals, washing dirty plates in readiness for the next relay of diners, while the three children carried the meals to the tables.

Hannes arrived in the kitchen with a tray of dirty crockery after the first sitting had finished, and said breathlessly, 'Guess what, Shelagh! *Mijnheer* and his wife have come to dinner!'

She said nothing, but stirred the gravy and mashed potatoes, and all the while the thought hammered in her head—*Luke has brought Diana. They're sitting on the* stoep, *bathed in romantic candlelight, talking and eating together. Why would a man take his wife to dinner unless there had been a degree of reconciliation between them?*

No matter what Diana had done in the past, the fact remained that she was a very beautiful woman. And Luke was a passionate and virile man. How could one blame him if he had succumbed to Diana's allure and her determination? He was, after all, irrevocably married to her.

He brought his wife to the farmhouse for dinner again the next night, and the next. Hannes informed Shelagh that he had asked for places to be permanently reserved for them. And the table he had chosen was in a secluded corner of the *stoep*, where the candlelight was very discreet and there was some degree of privacy.

Shelagh threw herself into the work of the eating-house, and tried not to think of Luke and Diana. Daily the pile of half-sovereigns which Hannes collected from the miners grew, and Shelagh was able to order table wine for her customers from one of the *smous*.

When Abel Dixon announced that he needed a temporary respite from the company of miners, and meant to visit Hopetown for a while, Shelagh took swift advantage of his departure and turned the room which he had been occupying into another public dining-room. Even then, there was always a patient line of miners waiting outside the house for free tables.

Shelagh guessed that at least part of her establishment's charm for the miners lay in its complete contrast with the daily life of the stinking, filthy encampment.

Conditions there were worsening by the day. The camp had acquired the name New Rush, to distinguish it from the river diggings, and daily the poor, the hopeful, the ambitious and the greedy continued to flock to it. The roughness and the danger, the foetid smell of corruption and the overpowering volume of noise kept the rich and the fastidious away.

The sound of pick and shovel, of bellowing oxen, of men shouting and swearing and quarrelling in a dozen different languages formed an unceasing background to daily life. Africans sang a strange haunting dirge as they hauled at the ropes which drew the leather buckets, filled with gravel to be sorted hopefully for elusive diamonds, to the surface of the ever-deepening pits.

Each little gang of registered licence-holder and his two or three African labourers dug away at its own pit, and as large numbers of these separate pits drove deeper and deeper into the bowels of the earth, problems and tempers flared.

Because no two gangs dug at the same rate, one pit might be anything up to twenty feet deeper than its next-door neighbour. When that happened, the owner of the deeper pit had to live with the constant danger that the walls of the pit next door might cave in upon him—and his labourers as they beavered away down below.

The yellow diamond-bearing ground was laboriously dug out of each claim into small leather buckets which were then hauled on to the access tracks by ropes, or by workers climbing up steps which had been hacked into the side of the pit. At the top, the gravel was poured from the buckets on to the pony-carts or wagons, and when the load was full of excavated gravel the conveyance was driven to the outskirts of the workings. Here the soil was sluiced through with water in a sieving cradle, the residue painstakingly sorted by hand on a trestle table.

The air was alive with ever-present tension, hostility and suspicion. It was so easy for someone to spy the dull gleam of a diamond in the flank of his neighbour's pit and to acquire it by swift sleight-of-hand. There were many opportunities for theft among the labourers, and buyers of stolen diamonds were beginning to establish a murky underground of crime on New Rush.

Working conditions in the mine were often appalling. In the same hour men labouring in the bowels of the earth could be smothered in choking dust and then drenched to the skin in a cloudburst.

When her customers began to forsake the eating-house Shelagh thought, at first, that the miners' preoccupation with their increasing daily difficulties had something to do with it. It was Luke who informed her of the truth.

She met him by the well one morning, and she was sharply and painfully aware of the fact that she was looking her very worst. Incarcerated in the kitchen for most of the day and for the whole of each evening, she had scarcely bothered to do more, lately, than pull a brush through her hair and tie it in a bun in her neck, and she wore Maria's oldest, dowdiest made-over gowns.

'Well, Shelagh,' Luke said, 'you've had a good run for your money, but your customers are deserting you in droves, and you'll soon have to close the eating-house. *Now* will you let me dig up your vegetable-patch?'

She looked at him with suddenly-aroused suspicion. 'What have you said to them, Luke? Is *that* why you and Diana have been haunting the eating-house so faithfully each evening—to undermine me?'

He said impatiently, 'The only reason we've been eating out is because it's cheaper than buying produce from the *smous* and cooking it oneself. Your meals are underpriced, Shelagh.'

It doesn't explain, she thought with pain, *why you choose the most discreet position on the* stoep, *as if you can't bear that other men should look at Diana . . .*

Aloud, she said, 'If my meals are underpriced, then why am I losing customers? Why should I be in danger of having to close the eating-house?'

'You have competition,' Luke said shortly. 'An

Irishman named Malone has started a rival eating-house out towards du Toit's Pan. His prices are much higher than yours and the food is inferior, but Malone provides the means of making the miners forget, for a few hours, the crude ugliness of their daily lives. He has brought in a second-rate pianist to entertain the customers while they eat.'

Shelagh was thoughtful as she walked away. It had never occurred to her that her customers might hunger for more than good food. But Luke was right, of course; they *did* need something to blur and soften the stark realities of their day-to-day existence . . .

By the time she had reached the house, Shelagh had made up her mind. She counted the hoard of half-sovereigns they had earned so far, and then called the three older children together.

'We'll have to make changes if we are to survive. I can't bring in a pianist, like Malone, so I've thought of another way of attracting the miners. I'm going to give them something to look at while they eat. Hannes, will you take the pony-cart and drive to the Griqua settlement? We need to hire a woman who can cook.'

The woman Hannes brought back was fat and cheerful and had an unpronounceable name, so that Shelagh compromised with its nearest equivalent and called her Nadine. By means of mime, because Nadine understood neither English nor Afrikaans, Shelagh explained what she wanted done, and was pleasantly surprised by the woman's quickness to learn.

While Nadine was preparing dinner for the evening, Shelagh spent the rest of the day in preparations of her own. Her gown of rose-coloured foulard was retrieved from the trunk in which it had been packed away, and when she had washed and dried her dark red hair she scooped it up and allowed it to fall in soft ringlets from the top of her head to her shoulders.

Each table was occupied as usual that evening when it became time to serve dinner. Only by the absence of more miners waiting for a second sitting could one measure the falling-off of custom.

Shelagh waited until Hannes, Dirkie and Rina had carried in the first course, and then she made her appearance.

She was a sensation from the moment the men first clapped eyes on her. Trying hard not to feel self-conscious, she moved slowly from table to table, enquiring whether everything was to her customers' liking, passing the time of day, allowing the men to feast their hungry eyes on her.

She was aware of the pounding of her heart and the high colour in her cheeks as she made her way to where Luke and Diana were sitting. In the candlelight Luke's eyes were dark hollows and his face had a gaunt appearance. Was he remembering, Shelagh wondered, the first time he had seen her wear the rose-coloured foulard gown at the river diggings, when he had ripped its bodice in an intentionally savage display of passion?

He rose suddenly, and said in a harsh voice, 'I'm not hungry after all, and there is something I have to do. Excuse me.'

So he *did* remember, Shelagh thought, and he

couldn't bear the reminder. Or—was it simply anger that had caused him to leave, because she was fighting back and he still couldn't persuade her to allow him to excavate her vegetable-patch?

Shelagh was about to walk on, but Diana said, 'Why don't you sit down for a moment?'

Because the eyes of everyone were upon them, Shelagh complied. 'I can see what you're trying to do,' Diana said frankly. 'You're fighting back at Malone, competing by bringing a little glamour into the lives of the miners. Personally, I hope you won't succeed.'

'Oh?'

'I would have to stop coming here if you did. You're bound to inflame passions by showing yourself off like this each evening, and there'll be brawls between your admirers. You and your eating-house would become somewhat notorious. I couldn't have my name associated with the kind of place this would become.'

Shelagh stared at her in astonishment. This was the woman who had conducted an affaire with her footman while she was, at the same time, the mistress of a royal duke! The woman who had rocked London Society with public scandal!

Diana understood Shelagh's thoughts, for she smiled. 'I have to be like Caesar's wife from now on. Many of the people grubbing here in the dirt for diamonds will become millionaires and move up in the world; they'll take their fortunes to London and become accepted on the fringes of Society. They will remember me and they'll talk. What they must remember is a dignified, fastidious gentlewoman who helped those less fortunate than herself, but who kept herself aloof from anything that was fast or questionable or in dubious taste.'

'You—plan very far ahead,' Shelagh said helplessly.

'Not that far ahead,' Diana contradicted. 'Luke is becoming discouraged. Other people are making fortunes, while he finds only just enough stones to enable him to get by. I don't think it will be very long before he'll be persuaded to pull out and go back to England, become reconciled with his family and go into his father's export business.'

So many questions burned on Shelagh's tongue. She wanted desperately to ask Diana whether she and Luke had become reconciled, but because she was afraid of the answer, she excused herself and began to circulate among the diners once more.

After that evening her former customers returned in droves. True to her word, Diana deserted the eating-house, and it stabbed like a knife-wound in Shelagh's heart that Luke, too, stayed away. It could only have been out of loyalty and support for his wife.

Abel Dixon returned from Hopetown wearing a new, expensive gold watch and chain, and a frock-coat which must have been imported into the country at vast cost. He had obviously been spending most of the rent-money he had so far received.

His face flushed with anger when he learnt that there was no longer a room available for him in the farmhouse. He made several veiled threats about leaving the country and taking the children with him, but Shelagh guessed that, until his next rental of a thousand guineas became due, he would be hard put to it to travel anywhere by himself, let alone to England with three children.

He obtained lodgings in one of the rooming-houses which had sprung up in New Rush, and most evenings he came to the farmhouse to eat. He would sit and listen with barely concealed envy to the tales of the miners around him, to their talk of lucky strikes and blue stones of the highest quality, and Shelagh could almost see his thoughts at work, trying to explore possible new ways of enriching himself at the diggings.

Winter arrived, bringing with it new hardships for the miners. Hard frost made digging difficult and the ground more reluctant to give up its diamonds. Shelagh, who was allowing her vegetable-patch to lie fallow and was supplementing the produce she had stored with what she could buy from the *smous*, was aware that Luke was casting his covetous eyes on it, and waited for him to approach her yet again with arguments for digging it up.

In that July, the miners of New Rush were given a much-needed boost to their morale. Three exceptionally large and fine stones were found on du Toit's Pan, on a hillock known as Colesberg Kopje. A native labourer of one Fleetwood Rawstone who leased the claim discovered them, and the fact that he was almost too drunk to see straight at the time merely added colour to the legend which immediately sprang up about the find.

The size and perfection of the diamonds discovered at Colesberg Kopje brought even more fortune-seekers seething into the area, and seemingly everyone wanted to eat at Shelagh's now-famous establishment.

One evening when she made her appearance, as usual, to circulate among the miners, she was galvanised by the sudden realisation that Luke had sat down at one of the tables. Diana was not with him.

Shelagh forced herself to give him a serene, welcoming smile as she moved towards him, exactly as if he were just another customer.

'You're a little late for the first course,' she said, 'but I'll see what can be arranged.'

'I want nothing to eat,' he interrupted tersely. 'Just send me a bottle of brandy-wine.'

Disturbed and concerned, Shelagh had no other course but to comply. And there he sat all evening, steadily drinking brandy-wine, his eyes holding a strange glitter as they followed Shelagh about the room.

Towards midnight all the customers had left save for Luke and a young man Shelagh knew as Harry. The latter had, for some weeks now, made a point of being the last customer to leave so that he could be sure of a few private words with her. She did not mind; Harry was young and lonely and love-lorn and did not pose any kind of threat.

But this evening it was clear that he meant to outstay Luke, and it was equally clear that Luke had no intention of being obliging enough to leave first. Indeed, his gaze was one of smouldering hostility as it rested on Harry.

Shelagh wondered uneasily how she was to

handle this impasse. The children had long since gone to bed and Nadine had finished in the kitchen and gone off duty. She was about to voice a humorous appeal to the two men when Luke suddenly got to his feet. In spite of the brandy-wine which he had been drinking, his gait was firm and steady as he walked towards Harry.

Unceremoniously, he took the other man by the collar and pulled him to his feet. '*Out*!' he snarled.

There was something so implacable in his face that Harry, whose first instinct had obviously been to square up to Luke, gave Shelagh an uncertain glance instead.

'*Please*,' she begged. 'I want no trouble. Please leave.'

'Are you sure you'll be safe?' Harry demanded. 'I could come back with a couple of the lads and see to this madman—'

'No, no! Please, just go. I'll be perfectly safe.'

He gave Luke a glare of dislike, and went to the door. Shelagh began angrily, as soon as he was out of earshot, 'How dared you! How dared you come here and get drunk—'

'I am not in the least drunk,' Luke interrupted tautly. 'I am merely sickened to the soul by the shameless display you make of yourself for the titillation of your customers!'

Shelagh drew a sharp breath of shock and outrage. Suddenly his hands were upon her forearms, hurting her, and his mouth against her hair. In a tortured voice, as though the words were being dragged from deep inside him, he went on, 'I knew I wouldn't be able to bear it. Their eyes devouring you, and knowing that I had no rights . . . That was why I stayed away. That was why I had to have a bottle of brandy-wine tonight. And even then it was not to be endured . . .'

Her heart was pounding in a painful rhythm. 'Luke,' she asked quietly, 'if—if you felt like that, why *did* you come tonight?'

He drew away from her. His eyes were flat and empty now, and his face had a gaunt look of defeat.

'I came to tell you that I'm finished.'

'What—whatever can you mean?'

'You know that I was the first to dig on Mooifontein, and therefore my excavations go deeper than those of any of the other miners. You also know, Shelagh, that the diamonds have been found embedded in vertical, volcanic pipes in the yellow ground. But what no one else besides me knows as yet is that underneath the yellow ground there is nothing but hard blue bedrock. I have reached that bedrock, Shelagh. There is not so much as an inch of yellow clay left on my claim, and therefore there is no further hope of my finding another solitary diamond. So I have come to the end of the road. I'm packing up and leaving.'

'Where—' she asked through numb lips, 'where would you go?'

He shrugged. 'Does it matter? Diana wants me to take her back to London, to make my peace with my family and enter my father's business. Since I'll never be rid of her, and since I no longer have the capital to go back to mining in India, I might as well do as she asks.'

'No!' Shelagh said fiercely. 'Don't give up hope! There's still my kitchen-garden. Dig it up!'

He shook his head. 'I haven't come here tonight to put unfair pressure on you. I know what your kitchen-garden means to you—'

'Measured against the possibility of never seeing you again, Luke, of knowing that we were separated by half a world, it means nothing at all! Dig it up!'

Gradually, she saw the hope return to his eyes. He drew her towards him and moved his lips very gently over hers in soft feathery little kisses which left her melting and aching inside. And because both of them knew that they would not be able to control the explosion of passion which would inevitably follow, Luke put her abruptly aside and left the house.

Dawn was just breaking the next morning when Shelagh was wakened by the sound of digging, and when she padded to the window she could see Luke and his two Griqua labourers at work in the vegetable-patch. She could not stifle a pang for the loss of it, and neither could she quell her still deeply-rooted instinct that it ought to have been left inviolate.

During the days that followed Luke and his men worked almost unceasingly. They continued until late into each night, working by the light of hurricane-lanterns.

One afternoon Shelagh suddenly became aware that the constant background of digging had stopped. Joy had recently begun to toddle and she took her by the hand to walk slowly towards the great chasm which had once been her kitchen-garden.

Luke was on the perimeter, staring down into the pit. He turned slowly as Shelagh and the baby approached.

'You were right,' he said dully, 'and I was wrong.'

'What do you mean, Luke?'

He began to laugh, a sound of bitter self-mockery and despair. 'There's not a trace of a diamondiferous pipe in the whole area. Your instinct was right all the time, Shelagh. I've torn up your vegetable-patch—deprived you and the children of a living—and all for nothing.'

CHAPTER TEN

IT WAS terrible to witness Luke's defeat. He allowed himself and his Griqua labourers only one afternoon's respite, and then the three of them began, laboriously, to fill in the chasm which they had made of Shelagh's kitchen-garden.

Red top-soil, black shale, melaphyne and quartzite, all were shovelled back into the hole and the ground made level once more.

'It will no longer become a catchment-area when it rains,' Luke told Shelagh bleakly. 'But I'm afraid nothing will grow there again for years.'

'It doesn't matter,' she said in a gentle voice. 'I've saved almost all of the profits from the eating-house. I'll buy provisions from the *smous*, and stay in business by putting up my prices. But you, Luke—what will you do now? Will you be returning to England after all?'

'How could I do that?' he responded wearily. 'How could I go away, not knowing whether you and the children will starve because of what I've done?' He stared into the distance. 'No, somehow I must keep going here. There are a few other prospectors with half-worked claims who are admitting defeat. I'll take over their claims if I can think of a way of beating the rapacious Abel Dixon down on the rental.'

Shelagh happened to be present when he confronted Dixon. The latter had been eating at the farmhouse one evening, when Luke arrived and asked him to stay on after the other diners had left, as he wished to discuss a business matter.

In the hope of clouding Dixon's judgment, or at least putting him in a receptive mood, but also to do whatever she could to boost Luke's morale, Shelagh brought out a bottle of wine and at the invitation of Luke, she joined the two men.

'In your own interests far more than in mine,' Luke addressed the other man bluntly, 'what I have to tell you had better go no further. The truth is that I've discovered once the yellow clay has been exhausted, there is nothing but hard blue bedrock waiting underneath.'

'What does that mean?' Dixon demanded.

'It means, quite simply, that once the bedrock has been reached there are no diamonds left. I've reached that bedrock on my claim. So now, just to keep going, I want to take over some half-worked claims from other prospectors. But I can't pay your fancy prices—'

'Sorry, old chap. You know my terms—'

'And I'm now about to tell you mine,' Luke interrupted him firmly. 'Lower your terms to me, and let me take over the half-worked claims at a nominal price. If you don't—well, I shall see to it that every prospector paying your rental fees learns the truth. They'll throw in their hands and move on, and there'll be no further rich monthly sums dropping into your lap.'

Dixon's eyes narrowed. 'How do I know that you're telling the truth?'

'You're welcome to have a look at my claim and see for yourself,' Luke said with a shrug. 'You'll find that there is no way of cutting through the hard bedrock.'

Dixon capitulated then, and by means of what amounted virtually to blackmail Luke acquired a few more half-worked claims which enabled him to keep going—for the immediate future, at any rate.

Luke stayed on for a while after Abel Dixon had taken his leave. He clasped Shelagh's wrist in his hand, and looked into her eyes.

'I love you,' he said quietly. 'I want you to remember that. Even if we can never be together, Shelagh, I want you to know that you are constantly in my thoughts, from my first waking moment until I fall asleep at night. I may be married to Diana, but my love and my loyalty belong to you.'

'Luke—' She swallowed painfully. 'It's—an unrealistic way of going on. I wouldn't blame you if—' She stopped, and continued—'I have sometimes wondered whether you have resumed sharing Diana's bed—'

'Good God, no!' he ground out with revulsion. 'What put that thought into your head?'

'Well—you used to take her to dinner, and sit in the most secluded spot—'

'I've told you, the reason we dined out was because it was cheaper, and because Diana is no cook. And the reason why we sat in a secluded spot was because she didn't want the miners to stare at her. My wife, after years of revelling in drawing attention to herself, has suddenly become a modest shrinking violet.'

Shelagh had always disliked discussing Luke's wife with him, but now she felt impelled to explain, 'Diana is hoping to redeem herself in the eyes of London Society.'

'I know. She continues to cling to the misguided hope that I'll go back there with her.' He swore despairingly under his breath. 'If only she would accept that she'll never change my mind on that after what I've done by digging up your kitchen-garden. Perhaps, then, she would run off with someone else instead!'

Shelagh tried to smile. 'I can't think of anyone at the diggings with whom Diana would stoop to run away.'

'No, unfortunately. So she continues to behave as virtuously as a nun, and I swear she has the patience of one, or she would not otherwise have been able to resign herself for so long to living in this hell-hole!'

But there was nothing nun-like about Diana when she called at the farmhouse, later, and raged at Shelagh. 'Why did you ever allow Luke to dig up your land? Oh damn you, Shelagh Maybury! He was on the point of giving up, I know, and I'm sure I could have persuaded him to take me to London! And then you ruined everything by interfering! Now he says we must stay here, because he feels responsible for you and the children!'

'If he had found diamonds,' Shelagh began, 'you would have been pleased enough—'

'*Diamonds!*' Diana exploded. 'I'm sick to the soul with talk about diamonds, with men endlessly grubbing in the dirt for diamonds, gambling everything on the hope of finding diamonds!' Diana's face was contorted, so that she looked almost ugly at that moment. 'And I'll tell you something else, Shelagh Maybury! I won't forget that *you* were the one who ruined my chance of getting out of here! You'll never have Luke—*never!* Even if I should have no more use for him one day, I'll still keep him from you!'

Shelagh was too shaken by this virulent display to say anything. At the door, Diana turned, her eyes narrowed with malice.

'He might hanker after you romantically, because you're unattainable. But he is a man, when all is said and done, with all of a normal man's needs. And I am in the best possible position to seduce him if I should decide to do so. Remember that whenever you feel like congratulating yourself on keeping him here!'

Shelagh winced, and coloured, and then felt something like contemptuous pity for Diana as she remembered Luke's revulsion at the mere suggestion that he might have been tempted to share his wife's bed.

With only Luke, Shelagh and Abel Dixon aware of the fact that the diamond-workings were reaching the point of exhaustion, blind optimism boomed elsewhere. As more and more stones were found on neighbouring farms, big business moved into the area. Mooifontein's neighbouring farm, du Toit's Pan, was sold to a syndicate over the heads of the diggers who were leasing mining rights. The various tented cities which sprawled over all the different farms grew and expanded until they merged as one. The time had come for the rough mining town to be named.

During a meeting of the Diggers' Committee, the matter was put to the vote, and it was decided to call the mining town after the first Earl of Kimberley, the Secretary of State for the Colonies.

Kimberley was a mellifluous, pretentious name for an ugly conglomeration of tents and shacks whose occupants were continually at the mercy of dysentery, typhus and camp-fever. A place with no water-supply other than Shelagh's well, a place with no sanitation, where its citizens wallowed in mud when the rains came or choked in dust under a harsh and pitiless sun. A place where men grubbed like insects in the vast honeycomb of holes in the ground, and fought and got drunk or spent their money in the whore-houses when the day was over.

As more and more of the other prospectors around Shelagh reached the hard blue bedrock on their claims, miners began to pull out. The dishonest ones shovelled back worked-out yellow earth to cover the bottom of their pits and sold out to innocent, unwary newcomers; the more honourable simply abandoned their claims and moved on. When this happened, Luke would acquire the claims at a greatly reduced rental from an enraged Abel Dixon.

The latter came and complained to Shelagh

about it, as though it were somehow her responsibility. 'That man is taking the bread and butter from the mouths of the children!' he declared bitterly.

'I don't recall any bread and butter being forthcoming from all the rents you've collected over the months,' Shelagh pointed out.

'I was talking figuratively! The money has all been safely invested for the children. But the Lord knows, I've had so many expenses in my capacity as their guardian . . . And now Luke Valentine is forcing me to accept rock-bottom rentals and there is not a thing I can do about it, for none of the syndicates will buy the land now that it has become known the yellow ground is almost worked out.'

He sighed. 'The strain of it all is making me ill. I suffer from the most dreadful palpitations, and I have a troublesome headache which I'm sure is a symptom of something far more serious—'

Rina looked up from where she was playing with Joy on the floor, and said innocently, 'Ma once knew someone who had a headache come on one evening, and in the morning he was dead.'

Abel Dixon shuddered, and left the farmhouse. Shelagh hid a smile, and then sighed as she thought of Luke—taking over worked-out claims, picking through second-hand rubble in the hope of finding diamonds previously missed—and all just to keep going.

She couldn't help being struck by one of the newcomers to Kimberley who occasionally came to eat at the farmhouse. It was not that he was particularly prepossessing in a physical sense, for he had a pale complexion, a large nose and a squeaky voice, and he soon made it clear that he had a dislike of women. But there was something magnetic about him, a nervous energy and enthusiasm which impressed Shelagh in one so young, for she learnt that he was only nineteen years old.

His name was Cecil Rhodes, and he shared a claim with his brother. The two of them did no better out of it than any of the other miners who had not been lucky enough to strike it rich with some huge stone, but Shelagh was not in the least surprised when she learnt that young Cecil Rhodes was earning money, in the meantime, by selling water and ice from an imported machine to the other diggers. He was, she decided, an enterprising youth who would go far.

The next new arrival at Kimberley to claim her attention could not have been in sharper contrast with Cecil Rhodes. He arrived riding a mule, with his possessions strapped behind him, and Shelagh watched him making for the farmhouse. As he slid from the back of the animal to open the gate, she realised by his lurching movements that he was unwell, and she hurried to meet him.

To her astonishment, she recognised him as Dr Paul, from the river diggings. He was the man who had been indirectly responsible for the way in which her life had turned out, for it had been he who had directed her father's footsteps towards Mooifontein and Maria Steenkamp.

If Dr Paul had looked seedy and disreputable to Shelagh then, he had obviously plumbed new depths of degradation in the interval. His clothes were more markedly soiled than before, and he obviously slept in them. It was abundantly clear, too, that he was not ill so much as suffering from the effects of bad liquor.

Because he had done his best to help her father once, Shelagh took him into the house and fed him.

'Dear child, dear child,' he muttered, gazing at her through watery eyes. 'If I may further presume on your kindness, and ask for a little drink—?'

She hesitated, and then went to fetch a glass of wine. The poor man obviously needed it as much as he needed food.

'Have you come to rent a claim at Kimberley?' she asked as she sat down to keep him company.

He smiled ruefully. 'I am no longer in a physical condition to dig for diamonds. No, I hope to peddle my medical services among the miners instead.'

'It's true that there is no other doctor at the diggings,' she said doubtfully, 'and it's also true that there is a lot of sickness, but—'

'But you doubt if any reliance would be placed upon my ability as a doctor,' he finished for her with sad dignity. 'I hope to rehabilitate myself here. It will be my last chance.'

'I wish you all the luck in the world,' Shelagh said warmly. 'And that reminds me—I recall that my father forgot to pay you for the last of the physic you prescribed for his cough. I insist on settling that debt now.'

His dignity did not waver as he accepted both the lie and the sovereign which Shelagh pressed on him. He left the farmhouse to look for lodgings, and she could only hope that he would succeed in rehabilitating himself.

The trouble was that the people in Kimberley who became ill and needed medical attention were the very ones who could not afford to pay for it. The lucky ones, the ones who found diamonds and sold them to the dealers and to passing merchants, could afford to eat well and live reasonably comfortably in tin shacks instead of tents, and so they had in-built resistance to disease.

As she worried about Dr Paul, a happy thought suddenly struck Shelagh. Abel Dixon, with his morbid preoccupation with his own health, would make an ideal corner-stone for the practice which Dr Paul hoped to start in Kimberley!

She introduced the two men, and thereafter would often see them in consultation. But it was not Shelagh, nor Abel Dixon, who was ultimately responsible for Dr Paul's rehabilitation. It was, astonishingly enough, Diana Valentine.

As soon as she learnt of the presence of a doctor in Kimberley, Diana sent for him. Not long after that she began to organise a series of fund-raising events in Kimberley; the proceeds were to be used for a medical centre at which help would be freely available to the sick and the poor.

A corrugated-iron construction was set up, and there Dr Paul, his clothes still shabby but now clean, would hold a surgery each morning. Diana, looking chastely beautiful in a plain, high-necked gown, would assist him. Such was the respect she commanded from the miners that there was no shortage of voluntary contributions to pay for the medical centre and provide Dr Paul with a modest income. Diana steadfastly refused to accept a penny for her services.

She was indefatigable. When she was not helping Dr Paul minister to patients or organising fund-raising events to pay for new equipment, she was visiting the poor and the sick. She became known to everyone as the Angel of Kimberley.

Shelagh and Luke had met at the well one afternoon when they chanced to see Diana go by on one of her missions of mercy, carrying a hamper. As she progressed along the filthy, stinking streets, men touched their caps to her and women curtsied. She acknowledged their salutations with gracious but aloof dignity.

Luke glanced at Shelagh, a sick expression in his eyes. 'The Angel of Kimberley . . . If only they knew what a sham it all was, and how heartily she despises them! If only they could hear what she has to say about them in private!'

'She is creating quite a reputation to take with her when she returns to London,' Shelagh agreed quietly. 'A correspondent for a British newspaper called at the farmhouse yesterday, asking questions about her.'

Luke shook his head in a baffled way. 'She knows that it becomes more and more unlikely each day that I'll be forced to take her back to London. Apart from my commitment towards you and the children, she is aware that some of the claims I've taken over are yielding diamonds, albeit in modest quantities. And yet she works single-mindedly at her image as the Angel of Kimberley . . .'

'Some good is coming out of it,' Shelagh comforted him. 'The poor and the sick *are* being helped, and Dr Paul—apart from a few lapses—has become as sober and responsible as it's possible for him to be.'

He nodded, and then his brooding gaze upon her told Shelagh that he was no longer thinking of Diana. 'You were eighteen when I first clapped eyes on you,' he said abruptly. 'You appeared in the path of my mules, with the wind moulding your gown to your body, and I thought you looked like the figurehead on the prow of a ship . . .'

'I remember,' she said softly.

'Four years ago, and nothing has changed.' There was desperation in his voice. 'I still love you, and I still haven't found the fortune that will free me of Diana. Sometimes I wonder if anything *will* ever change.'

She knew what he meant, and yet it seemed absurd to talk of nothing having changed. The children had changed and grown in confidence. Now that their lives were no longer bound by farm chores, there was time for them to learn to read and write, and they were doing well at the lessons Shelagh set for them. Joy had changed from a puny scrap of humanity to a toddler with a lively, enquiring mind.

And daily, almost, Kimberley was changing too. Because of the depth of the honeycomb of pits in what had become known as the Big Hole, and because of the dangers of landslides, miners were no longer able to cart their excavated ore over bridges crossing other claims.

Instead, each man was forced to incur the expense of a long areal wire running from the perimeter to the bottom of his claim. Inside the pit a bucket was filled with ore; far above on the surface, horses and mules padded around great wooden wheels called whims, and the turning wheels shortened the wire and brought the bucket jerking up to the surface for sorting.

The effect of all these thousands of wires running from the perimeter, crossing and criss-crossing one another, was of a huge spider's web suspended over the Big Hole.

Everyday life in Kimberley was changing too. It was becoming more violent, more expensive. Every single article required by the diggers had to be carted nearly seven hundred miles from Cape Town, mostly by ox-wagon. Shelagh was now forced to charge the miners for drawing water at her well in order to make ends meet. The days when she served fresh green vegetables from her garden were now just a wistfully recalled memory.

Expensively bought cabbage or carrots made only an occasional appearance at her dinner-table, and at other times the children went out to gather from the veld certain wild plants which Shelagh cooked and served as vegetables.

Crime was on the increase, and illicit diamond-buying threatened everyone involved in the mining of the stones.

'Unless we can control it,' Luke explained to Shelagh, 'it will destroy the delicately poised market, and the price of diamonds will fall to rock-bottom.'

As it was, half the stones dug up each day were estimated to be stolen and would find their way on to the illicit market. The traffic invariably started with a dishonest African labourer who would hide a stolen diamond in a gap between his teeth, or in his hair. Then it was passed on to a receiver in Kimberley, and a native runner would slip away from the diggings to deliver the stone to an outside entrepreneur who was financing the whole project.

Vigilantes appointed by the Diggers' Committee searched everyone leaving Kimberley, but still stolen diamonds slipped through. Feelings regarding illicit diamond-buying ran so high that the mere suspicion of a man's being involved in it could lead to bloodshed.

Violence of all kinds, bred by the squalor of the conditions, became part of life at Kimberley, and it was not unusual to hear the sound of gunshots reverberating through the mining town. Shelagh worried about the effects of all this upon the children, and tried to create, within the farmhouse, an oasis of sanity and normality to counteract it.

Then something happened which drove all other fears and preoccupations from her consciousness. Dr Paul arrived at the farmhouse one morning, looking anxious and harassed.

'My dear Miss Maybury,' he said, 'I wonder if you would be so very kind as to assist me in my clinic this morning? It wouldn't be proper for me to examine female patients without a chaperon, and Mrs Valentine feels too unwell to carry on.'

'Yes, certainly,' Shelagh said, and enquired politely, 'What is wrong with Mrs Valentine?'

'Well—umm—' Dr Paul coughed discreetly. 'Nothing is *wrong*, precisely. It is merely her condition which is causing her to feel unwell.'

Shelagh felt as if she had just been pole-axed. She clung to the back of a chair for support, and heard herself ask in a far-away voice—

'Are you—saying—that she is expecting a baby?'

'Yes, indeed.' Dr Paul beamed at her, quite unaware of the mortal blow he had struck her. 'Shall we go, Miss Maybury?'

CHAPTER ELEVEN

As SHE followed the doctor to his corrugated iron clinic, jumbled thoughts pounded through Shelagh's brain.

She remembered Diana saying, '*Luke is a man, with all of a normal man's needs, and I am in the best possible position to seduce him.*'

And then Luke's words echoed in her ears. '*I love you, Shelagh. I may be married to Diana, but my love and my loyalty belong to you . . .*'

I can't bear it, she thought. I've borne too much during the years while I've loved him without hope, but this is—this is more than flesh and blood can be expected to endure . . .

As if to drive home the new anguish which she was being asked to accept, Luke was coming through the gate on his way to the well when Shelagh and Dr Paul approached. She stood in numb silence, staring at the ground, and heard the doctor say, 'I have sent your wife home, Mr Valentine, as she was not feeling quite the thing, but there is no cause for alarm.'

'I daresay she has caught a chill.' Luke's voice was polite.

Dr Paul made a sound of embarrassment. 'My

dear sir—can it possibly be that you don't know?'

'Know *what*?'

Shelagh looked up then, and said tonelessly, 'Diana is expecting a child.'

Luke stood there for a moment, his face totally blank. Then his eyes darkened with an expression of such murderous intensity that Shelagh instinctively shrank back. His lips drew away from his teeth in what was almost an animal snarl.

'By God, I don't know what game she is playing now, but she'll not get away with it!'

'My dear sir . . . my dear sir . . .' Dr Paul murmured in agitation.

Luke took him by the lapels, and hauled the doctor savagely towards him. 'You spend more time with her than anyone else! You must know what is behind this!'

'I—I can understand why your wife has not told you of her condition if this is your reaction to it . . . My dear sir, the matter is quite simple. There is nothing behind it, other than that you will be a father in some six months' time—'

Luke released Dr Paul, so that he almost fell. 'Not me,' he said with an ugly laugh. 'I presume you're sure of your facts, since you're a medical man. *But if Diana is having a baby, it is not mine!*'

Shelagh addressed the doctor quietly. 'Go on without me. I shall follow shortly.' When he had hurried thankfully away, she turned to Luke.

'I know—' she began with difficulty. 'I have always been fully aware—that the temptations must be overwhelming, living together as you do. So I—I cannot blame you—'

'Shut up!' He grabbed her by the shoulders, shaking her roughly. 'If that bitch is having a child, it is not mine!'

'Luke—be reasonable. No one else could be involved. You said, yourself, that she was behaving like a nun—'

'It is not mine, Shelagh!'

His passionately raised voice, his air of barely controlled savagery were attracting a small crowd. He seemed oblivious of the fact. He turned away from Shelagh and ploughed through the crowd. A little later she watched, appalled, as he stood in the doorway of the dwelling which he had erected for himself and Diana, and flung his wife's belongings out into the dusty street.

Diana, looking immensely dignified but pale, appeared and gathered her bags together. Several men rushed forward to help her. As if caught in a nightmare, Shelagh saw that one of the men had struck a blow at Luke and was, himself, sent sprawling in the dust by Luke's powerful fist.

Diana affected not to be aware of the ugliness of what was happening, but followed the men who were carrying her bags towards the medical centre.

The news of what had happened swept through Kimberley like wildfire. Luke was universally vilified and condemned. Someone tried to burn down his dwelling, and several threats were made against his life.

The Angel of Kimberley, on the other hand, received nothing but sympathy. People vied with one another to offer her hospitality, but she chose to take lodgings in the house in which Dr Paul lived so that he could be at hand if she should need his services in an emergency.

Feelings were running so high about the matter that there was no knowing what might have happened if Fate had not intervened to distract the miners.

One oppressively hot afternoon Shelagh was in the kitchen, trying to contain her anguished thoughts and give her mind, instead, to planning the evening's dinner with Nadine, when Hannes came bursting in.

'Shelagh,' he gasped, 'something awful has happened! The diggers at the centre of the Big Hole have tapped an underground water-table, and the mines are flooding!'

As if to drive home some obscure moral point, Fate compounded the flooding by causing the heavens to open later that same afternoon, and the rain drummed down upon what had become an immense catchment-area. The base of the Big Hole was turned into a muddy quagmire, and then into a turgid lake.

Mining stopped. There was no time to do anything but bale water out frantically by hand, which proved to be wasted effort, for the water rose more quickly than it could be collected in buckets.

In despair, seeing the end of the mine as a workable proposition, many of the miners moved out. Young Cecil Rhodes left, too, and even in the midst of her despair Shelagh was disappointed to see him go, for she had expected greater tenacity from him. Wasn't he for ever talking of the day when diamonds would be instrumental in colonising the African continent for the glory of the British Empire? And at the first major setback he had admitted defeat . . .

She had underestimated him, however. Before long he returned to Kimberley with a steam-driven pump which he hired out to the diggers. The latter were able to pump out their claims, and Rhodes used the money to take over other claims which had been abandoned. In this he was rivalled by Luke, who delighted Abel Dixon by offering the original high rents for the claims in order to outbid Rhodes.

'Why is Luke doing this?' Shelagh questioned Dixon anxiously when he came to dinner. She had caught only an occasional glimpse of Luke, looking tense and strained, since the day when he had thrown Diana and her belongings out of their home.

'I don't know,' Abel Dixon returned cheerfully. 'I think both he and Cecil Rhodes are quite mad. And there's another young man who has been buying up old claims. Barney Barnato is his name.'

Shelagh knew Barney Barnato. A former circus worker, he had arrived at Kimberley, penniless. Now he was working as a pedlar, buying up anything and everything he could obtain at favourable prices from the wagons which set out from Cape Town and re-selling at a modest profit to the miners.

He appeared to be a shrewd young man, and Cecil Rhodes had already proved himself to be one. So what were they about, together with Luke, buying up abandoned claims in this wholesale manner?

It was well known that the profitable life of the Big Hole was all but over now that the hard slate-blue formation was being reached. And yet these three men were falling over themselves to acquire yet more areas of useless worked-out craters and fruitless rubble. Whatever the motives of Rhodes and Barnato might be, Shelagh could not help fearing that Luke's mind had been affected by the tangible hostility which faced him daily.

For herself, no matter how she strove to close her own mind to it, the fact of Diana's pregnancy remained like an open wound in Shelagh's breast.

If it had been at all possible or reasonable, she would have clutched at the theory that Dr Paul was Diana's lover. But it simply could not have been. A woman like Diana would not have looked twice at a broken-down middle-aged doctor who drank himself into oblivion whenever the pressures of life grew too strong for him.

And there simply wasn't anyone else. Diana, carefully building up her shattered reputation, *had* lived like a nun.

The truth was inescapable. Luke had succumbed to almost unbearable temptation, and he could not face the consequences of his weakness, could not acknowledge to himself that it had happened.

Shelagh watched him growing haggard, his face hard-bitten as he defied public opinion and continued to reject Diana and the child she was carrying.

As for Diana, she remained dignified and true to her image as the Angel of Kimberley as she moved through the settlement on her errands of mercy, her waistline gradually thickening and her gait becoming slower and more deliberate.

A new crisis suddenly hit Kimberley. Shafts in the Big Hole were collapsing and the diggers were now working under constant threat of death. A system had to be evolved to avoid landslips, and all other work ceased as the miners gave their attention to the problem.

The Diggers' Committee called a meeting at the farmhouse one evening in an attempt to find a solution. In between serving the men with refreshments, Shelagh listened as various suggestions were made for fighting the collapse of the shafts. She saw Luke's gaze upon her, and when she met his eyes she could clearly read the angry, insistent message which they flashed at her.

'Diana's baby is not mine!'

At that precise moment Dr Paul came flying into the house in a state of great agitation.

'Mr Valentine—your wife—' he gasped.

'Yes?' Luke stared at him, stolid and apparently unmoved. Only a muscle jerking in his cheek betrayed his tension.

'Complications have arisen—something with which I do not have the facilities to cope! She will have to be taken to Hopetown immediately—'

'Then take her.' Luke's words fell like stones into the silence.

'I—Yes, well . . . Naturally, I intend to travel with her. But I cannot drive a conveyance at the same time. You—'

Luke threw his head back in an attitude of challenge. 'Then let the true father of her child volunteer to drive her!'

A gasp met his words. The small, tense silence which followed was broken by Abel Dixon. 'I'll drive you to Hopetown, Dr Paul,' he said. He glanced round the room.

'If anyone is reading any significance into my offer, then it's the grossest of insults to Mrs Valentine. I am volunteering only because I alone among you am not needed here to cope with the problem of collapsing mine-shafts.'

He began to stride to the door and Dr Paul hurried to keep up with him. As if their departure had been a signal, the ugliest of scenes erupted inside the room. Like baying animals out for blood, the men turned on Luke. With his back to the wall, he drove his fists into the flesh of his attackers. But he could not possibly hold out against such a mob.

The children had been woken and appeared at the door, Rina and Joy weeping. Shelagh went to them, and cried frantically at the men, 'Stop! Please stop it!'

No one paid any attention to her. She tried to help Luke by hitting out at his attackers with anything she could lay hands upon, but was easily and unceremoniously pushed out of the way.

Just when she thought the mob would surely kill Luke, a tremendous noise reached them from outside, and simultaneously the house shook as if a giant hand had taken it by its foundations and rattled it.

The men froze, and stared at one another. Luke, and their frenzied blood-lust, were forgotten.

'*Landslide!*' somebody yelled, and then the room became galvanised as everyone tried to reach the door at once.

Shelagh tried to detain Luke, whose face was bleeding from a cut on the cheek, but he pushed her aside and hurried out too. Slowly, she followed, taking Hannes with her and telling Rina to stay with the other two children.

The whole of Kimberley was in the streets, running to see what had happened, and cries of shock reached Shelagh long before she and Hannes had arrived at the scene of the disaster.

The road had collapsed under the weight of the conveyance which was taking Diana, Dr Paul and Abel Dixon to Hopetown. Deep in the recesses of the Big Hole their figures lay sprawled like broken dolls among a hellish confusion of dying mules and splintered wood and metal.

By the light of naphtha flares the bodies were brought to the surface. Dr Paul was still alive, but Abel Dixon was dead, and so was Diana, both their necks broken. And as they hauled Diana's body to the surface the scene took on a grotesque, nightmarish quality which Shelagh thought she would never forget as long as she lived.

A metal spoke from the wagon had impaled itself in Diana's side, and as they laid her body on the ground and pulled out the spoke they were met not, as had been expected, by the sight of blood flowing from her side. The spoke had not penetrated her flesh, but had embedded itself in a heavy corset which she wore. And the reason why the spoke had not connected with her flesh was because the corset had been stuffed with diamonds.

The stones fell to the ground in a cascade of brilliance underneath the naphtha flares. Diamonds which had been stolen and hoarded and added to over the months as Diana's 'pregnancy' grew.

Dr Paul survived for long enough to tell the Diggers' Committee all the details of their devilishly cunning plan, and soon the whole of Kimberley knew what had happened.

Dr Paul and Abel Dixon and Diana, different from one another in almost every way, had yet had one common bond. All three of them had wanted money; all of them had wanted, ultimately, to escape from the hell of the diggings. And once they recognised their mutual ambition, they began to plot ways of bringing it about.

It was easy enough to buy stolen diamonds for a song in Kimberley. What was not simple was getting them out of the mining town in any quantity. But who would suspect a pregnant woman for whom there was enormous public sympathy, a pregnant woman who had to be rushed out of Kimberley because of complications in her condition? Who would be crass enough to suggest that she should be searched?

And to make quite certain that Abel Dixon would be the volunteer to drive the doctor and Diana out of Hopetown, it had been decided to wait for one of the all-too-frequent emergencies to erupt so that all the other men would be loath to leave their claims.

A week after the accident, when Dr Paul's

account had been pieced together and he had slipped into a coma from which he was not expected to recover, Luke called at the farmhouse to tell Shelagh the full story. It was late in the evening; the last diners had long since left, and the children were asleep.

'Diana knew I would throw her out,' he ended. 'The three of them banked on it. Not only because it increased public sympathy for her, but also because it would have been too difficult for her to sustain her growing "pregnancy" under my eyes.'

'She planned to return to England with the diamonds, of course . . .'

'Oh yes. If matters had gone smoothly there would have been a message for me from Hopetown, saying that the doctors there had been unable to help, and that she was going on to Cape Town. And then, I've no doubt, there would have been a further letter to say that she had lost the baby, and was returning to England. Once there, she gambled that her saintly reputation gained at Kimberley, helped by the vast fortune she hoped to realise from the sale of her share of the diamonds, would restore her to her former position in Society.'

Shelagh glanced at him, and looked away. 'I'm—sorry that I doubted you—'

He made a rough sound. 'No recriminations! We've already wasted too much time, too many years. Come here, Shelagh.'

She went slowly towards him. His arms closed about her and he pulled her down on the sofa . His lips touched her eyelids, and she shivered slightly as she felt them move along the trail of her cheek towards her mouth.

Her hands fumbled with the buttons of his shirt, and he made a lingering, tantalising business of unhooking each loop from its corresponding pearl-shaped fastening of her bodice, pausing to kiss the soft flesh exposed. Then his hands cupped her breasts, evoking a whimpering response from her as his fingers moved gently over the nipples.

He stretched out on the sofa, pulling her down with him so that their bodies fused closely, their mouths locking. And then he possessed her utterly, both mind and body, so that the long wasted years seemed to fall away as if they had never been.

A long while later, as he lay smoothing the hair away from her flushed face, he said almost casually, 'By the way, I forgot to tell you. We shall be enormously rich, you and I and the children.'

She smiled into his eyes. If she had ever had any doubts about his taking on the children, his casual inclusion of them in their joint future had dispelled them. Then the essence of what he had said struck her.

'Rich?' she repeated. 'You mean—the diamonds Diana tried to smuggle out—?'

'No, I don't mean that. For the sake of fairness they are being shared out equally among all the claim-owners.' He shifted his position to one of greater comfort, and went on. 'You know the blue bedrock which all the diggers have now reached? Well, it began to occur to me a while back that the hard blue ground could also be rich in diamonds. Since diamonds are created by a combination of heat and pressure, the deeper the vertical pipes from which they spring, the larger the stones should be. So, if there *were* diamonds in the blue ground, they would be bigger than anything we had yet dug up.'

'I see . . .' Shelagh murmured.

He paused to kiss the hollow of her throat. 'The question was, how to break up the hard blue ground? It seemed an insuperable problem. I'd hacked out a piece of bedrock to examine it more closely, and then all the problems about flooding and landslides claimed my attention and I left the piece of blue matrix lying out in the open, where it was first scorched by the hot sun and then soaked by the heavy rain and then sun-baked once more.'

He smiled triumphantly. 'When I remembered about it again, I found that the elements had obligingly solved the problem for me. The hard rock had crumbled away, exposing two perfect diamonds of considerable size and quality.'

'That's why you acquired all those abandoned claims!' Shelagh exclaimed.

'That was why. Barney Barnato and Cecil Rhodes had been arguing along the same lines.' Luke reached for her again, and added, 'So you had better start considering where in the world you and the children want us to make our home.'

'It doesn't matter,' Shelagh murmured as she moved her hands over the firm, taut flesh of his chest and offered him her mouth again. 'Nothing matters now.'

THE END